"I still don't know why you're doing this."

"Maybe you don't have to know why," Daniel said.

"That's a load of malarkey," Christine replied.

"Malarkey? That's not a word you hear every day."

"I have this daughter, you see. She has a tendency to pick up on words and repeat them loudly when it's most inconvenient."

She was looking at him again with both eyes now. "Why, Daniel?"

"I didn't want to be another person who let you down."

"I don't want you to be another person who lets me down," she said softly.

For too much of his life, he had been concerned with his own interests. It was in his best interests to keep his siblings protected and the family business solvent. But what did he have to gain from Christine? What was in it for him to shield Marie?

Nothing. He had nothing to gain by doing any of this.

Funny how that hadn't stopped him yet.

* * *

Billionaire's Baby Promise
is part of Mills & Boon Desire's Nº1 bestselling
series, Billionaires and Babies: Powerful men…
wrapped around their babies' little fingers.

BILLIONAIRE'S
BABY PROMISE

BY
SARAH M. ANDERSON

MILLS & BOON

First Published in Great Britain 2017
By Mills & Boon, an imprint of HarperCollins*Publishers*
1 London Bridge Street, London, SE1 9GF

© 2017 Sarah M. Anderson

ISBN: 978-0-263-06861-0

Our policy is to use papers that are natural, renewable and recyclable
products and made from wood grown in sustainable forests. The logging
and manufacturing processes conform to the legal environmental
regulations of the country of origin.

Printed and bound in Great Britain
by CPI Antony Rowe, Chippenham, Wiltshire

Sarah M. Anderson may live east of the Mississippi River, but her heart lies out west. *A Man of Privilege* won an *RT Book Reviews* 2012 Reviewers' Choice Best Book Award. *The Nanny Plan* was a 2016 RITA® Award winner for Contemporary Romance: Short.

Sarah spends her days talking with imaginary cowboys and billionaires. Find out more about Sarah's heroes at sarahmanderson.com and sign up for the new-release newsletter at eepurl.com/nv39b.

To Tahra Seplowin, who once pulled my luggage through Times Square at a dead run so we could make the curtain call. That's true friendship right there.

One

As always, he answered the phone on the first ring. "This is Daniel."

The number was not one he recognized. The voice, on the other hand, was. "Lee! I knew I'd track your sorry butt down somehow."

"Brian," Daniel said, trying to keep the cringe out of his voice.

Brian White had plucked Daniel straight out of a political rally on the campus of Northwestern and taught him everything he knew. They had worked together for almost fourteen years on various political campaigns. Brian was a man without morals, scruples or ethics. As a result, he had an amazing track record in getting questionable candidates elected to public office.

"How have you been?" Daniel asked, stalling for time.

If Brian was calling him now, that only meant one thing. The man had been hired to run yet another political campaign and he wanted his right-hand man by his side. Never mind that Daniel Lee had walked away from politics and made it clear that he was never going back.

"I've got a job for you," Brian said, sounding sure of himself.

It was hard to surprise Daniel Lee. He made secrets his business. So he wasn't all that surprised that Brian was reaching out to him. What did surprise him was his own physical response. Daniel—a man who was rumored by his political enemies to not even have a soul—felt an anxious coiling in his stomach that was only dimly recognizable as guilt. "I have a job, Brian."

"Doing what? Running a marketing department for a beer company? Come on, Lee. We both know you're wasting your talents."

Daniel rolled his eyes. Brian didn't know the first thing about business—or loyalty. Daniel wasn't just running a marketing firm for a beer company—he was running a family business. His last name might not be Beaumont, but he was one all the same.

Every time he thought of his position here at the Beaumont Brewery—second-in-command to his half brother, Zeb Richards—he almost wished his grandfather, Lee Dae-Won, could have lived long enough to see Daniel take his rightful place in a family business—even if it wasn't Dae-Won's business. "I told you I was out."

As he spoke, he started searching. Who was Brian working for now?

"Yeah, yeah—that's what you said. But you and I both know you didn't mean it. This one's going to be fun—carte blanche." There was a pause. "You find it yet?"

Damn. Of course Brian knew him well enough to know Daniel was already looking. "You could tell me," he said as he found it.

Missouri Senator Resigns In Disgrace; Male Escort Tells All.

Missouri? The hairs on the back of Daniel's neck stood up. Brian couldn't seriously mean...

"Clarence Murray wants to hire you to work on his campaign for a special election for the Missouri Senate seat recently vacated by the disgraced Senator Struthers." Somehow, Brian managed to sound enthusiastic.

It took a lot to surprise Daniel but for a moment, he was truly stunned.

"You've got to be kidding me." It hadn't even been two years since Daniel had destroyed Clarence Murray in a bid for the Missouri governor's office. "Murray is insane."

"However true that may or may not be, he has a lot of well-funded campaign donors." Brian's voice had leveled out, which was not a good sign.

"After what we did to him two years ago, you still think he's electable?" But even as he asked, Daniel knew how Brian would respond.

"It's not my job to decide if he's electable or not. He and his donors think he's electable, so it's my job to assemble a team and get him elected. That's where you come in."

Daniel kept searching. Murray, it seemed, had spent the better part of the last two years lying low and rebuilding his supporter base. Clarence Murray was a fire-and-brimstone preacher. He played well across the Bible Belt and had a solid evangelical base. But his beliefs were extreme and would never have a crossover appeal.

"No," he told Brian.

"Come on, Lee—it'll be fun. I'm already hearing whispers that Democrats think they can win this seat."

And then, there *she* was—halfway down the list of search results. Daniel recognized that headline—he had written it himself. He had chosen the picture of her because the angle was horrible and she looked like she had three extra chins. Seeing it again hit him like a punch to the gut.

Murray's Daughter Pregnant—Who Is The Baby Daddy?

Clarence Murray might have delusions of grandeur about being God's chosen politician. But in the end, it had been his pregnant daughter who had cost him the election. His pregnant, unmarried daughter.

Christine Murray.

Because Daniel was the one who had made her a campaign issue.

All was fair in love and war—and politics. For years, Daniel had played the game as well as anyone. Sometimes his candidates lost. More often than not, they won. Each time Daniel had worked a campaign, he'd gotten better at ferreting out secrets. And if candidates had few secrets, then Daniel had…well, not invented them. But he had always found some kernel of truth that could be stretched into something resembling a scandal. Nobody was completely clean.

Not even Daniel.

He read about Christine Murray, that anxious pit in his stomach coiling more tightly, a snake getting ready to strike. It didn't seem possible that he felt bad about what he had done. He never had before. But as he looked at the images of her online—and the headlines that he had *not* written about her—he had to face the fact that he had done a terrible thing to an innocent bystander.

"You know they're going to come after his daughter again."

As odd as it seemed now, it appeared that, at the advanced age of thirty-four, Daniel Lee had developed a conscience.

Christine Murray had been twenty-four years old when

her father had run for governor. From what Daniel had been able to dig up, she hadn't lived at home since she'd gone to college at the age of eighteen. She'd had a wild youth after the death of her mother—the stereotypical preacher's daughter—but by all appearances she had quickly settled down. She'd gotten a degree in finance. By all accounts, she had very little to do with Clarence Murray. Instead, she had gotten engaged and then gotten pregnant. By itself, there really wasn't anything scandalous about that.

Except that her father was running on a faith-and-family-values platform and having an unwed, pregnant daughter was exactly the sort of ammunition Daniel had needed to knock Clarence Murray out of the race.

Daniel had dragged that woman through the mud. When her fiancé had dumped her, Daniel had made hay while the sun still shone.

"I wouldn't worry about her," Brian said, sounding smug. "I have a plan. But I need you by my side. What do you say to one more—for old time's sake?"

Consciences were messy things. Daniel's stomach turned. No wonder he hadn't had one for so long.

Christine Murray stared at him from dozens of photos on his computer screen. Blonde, petite, curvy, with huge blue eyes—absolutely beautiful, except that, in all of the pictures, she looked like a wild deer that had been cornered by a pack of hungry wolves.

"Can't help you," Daniel told Brian. Because he couldn't. He hadn't felt bad about working to defeat Clarence Murray. The man was not fit to govern.

But Christine Murray?

"Lee, quit joking around. It's going to be a bloodbath and I need you by my side. No one can uncover secrets like you."

"Good luck with your candidate," he said. "But I'm out."

Brian hesitated. "Is it just because of Murray?"

"No. I'm out for good. Don't call me again."

"Is that an order?" Brian's voice got level again—which continued to be a bad sign. "Because I thought we were friends, Lee. I thought we had been friends for a long, long time."

Daniel was no idiot. He knew a threat when he heard one. And running a political campaign involved negotiating the ever-moving line between legal and illegal, ethical and unethical. Nobody cared about morals.

Brian's threat was empty, though. He couldn't very well throw Daniel under the bus without getting his own legs run over.

"I'll cheer you on from the sidelines." As Daniel said it, Christine Murray's trapped eyes continued to stare at him from the computer screen.

Two years ago he'd realized she was stunning. A man would have to be blind not to see it. But he had ignored the attraction then. He should be able to do the same now. Something as base and inconvenient as desire screwed things up. It always did.

"You're making a mistake, Lee."

"I have a business to run. But it's been good talking to you, Brian." And with that parting line, he hung up. Daniel tried to turn his attention back to the latest reports on the marketing campaign for the Beaumont Brewery's launch of a new craft beer. But for once, Daniel couldn't focus.

He found himself staring at pictures of Christine Murray as his mind spun out all of the possibilities. Naïvely, Daniel found himself hoping that her father's opponent would leave Christine Murray out of it. He went back to his search results. There wasn't much. There was an announcement that her child had been born, a daughter. There was a teaser article that suggested she was going to sign for the next season of *Ballroom Dancing With Superstars*—but that was from the previous season. Clearly, she hadn't.

After digging deeper, he found what he was looking for—a small bio with the standard headshot attached to the First City Bank of Denver's website. It had to be her—those blue eyes were unmistakable. She was a loan officer at the First City Bank. And she was in Denver? He'd been out of the game too long—he hadn't realized she was so close.

Christine had nothing to do with her father—especially not if she had been in Denver for the last year and a half. She might not get dragged into this special election.

But Daniel knew that wasn't how things worked. The opposition's campaign manager would size up the competition. It would take all of twelve seconds to dig up every piece of useful information he could on Clarence Murray and when he did, Christine would be at the top of that list.

They would come for her again.

Daniel didn't like guilt. And he shouldn't care.

But he stared at the small picture on the bank's website. She didn't look trapped in that photo. She looked cautious, though. She looked like a woman who believed putting any picture of herself on the internet was inviting abuse.

If Daniel had any faith in Clarence Murray actually being a spiritual man, he might try to convince himself that Murray would close ranks around his daughter, try to protect her.

But Brian White wouldn't allow that to happen. Christine Murray was a liability. Daniel was willing to bet large sums of money—and he had large sums of money to bet—that Brian would attack her first. He would make an example out of her to show that Clarence Murray did not engage in nepotism and stuck by his beliefs.

Daniel picked up the phone and dialed the executive office. "Yes?" his half brother, Zeb, said into the phone. "Do you have those numbers?"

Daniel absolutely should not get involved. But two well-funded, cutthroat political campaigns were about to descend upon Christine Murray. "Not yet. I need to be out of the office for a little bit—hopefully just a couple of hours, but it has the potential to become more involved."

Zeb was quiet for a moment. "Everything okay?"

They had a tenuous relationship that was part stranger, part boss, part brother. The familial bonds felt awkward for both of them. "It should be. But if it becomes more involved, I'll let you know."

Zeb chuckled. "Yeah, that was reassuring. Good luck."

"Luck has nothing to do with it."

Which didn't change the fact that he was going to need all the luck he could get.

Christine Murray looked longingly at the coffeepot in the break room. She needed something stronger than green tea, but she had learned the hard way that if she had coffee this late in the day and then nursed Marie at bedtime, the girl would be bouncing off the walls all night long.

Not that Marie would sleep, anyway. She was teething—again—and all Christine could do was cling to her sanity in a blind stumble toward the weekend, where she would at least get to nap when Marie went down in the afternoon.

It was days like today that she gave thanks that she was a loan officer instead of a teller. She'd always liked being a teller—the job had paid her way through college. But she did not have it in her today to be perky.

Tea in hand, she settled in at her desk and stared at her computer without really seeing anything. She allowed herself a moment of indulgence to think *what if*. What if Doyle, her fiancé, had stuck by her during her father's last campaign? What if they had gotten married like they planned? What if she had some help with Marie?

But if she was going to dream about the impossible, she might as well go all out. What if her mom hadn't died? What if her father hadn't been on a quixotic journey toward political office for the last fifteen years? What if she had grown up in a normal household with normal parents?

Her phone rang, snapping her out of her reverie where life was perfect and everybody got at least seven hours of sleep every night. "Thank you for calling First City Bank of Denver, this is Christine. How can I help you?"

"Good afternoon, Ms. Murray." Something in the man's voice set her teeth on edge. "We haven't been properly introduced but my name is Brian White and I'm calling on behalf of your father, Clarence Murray," he added, as if Christine could possibly forget who her father was.

She slammed the phone down before she even realized what she was doing. She would never forget the name of the man who had ruined her life.

Brian White had been a campaign manager for the opponent in her father's last attempt at higher office.

The phone rang again and she knew it was him. She didn't want to answer it but she was at work. There was a chance that someone was calling about a loan. So, squeezing her eyes shut, she answered.

"Ms. Murray—I believe we were disconnected."

The bottom fell out of her stomach and she sat bolt upright at her desk. "What do you want?"

"Ms. Murray. There is no need to sound alarmed," he

went on in that slick voice, which of course only scared her more. "Your father has asked me to reach out to you."

"Oh?" Her voice wavered, darn it all. "He couldn't bother to call me himself, I guess? I'm only his daughter, right?"

Mentally, she high-fived herself. She was still getting used to standing up for herself. She was not going to cower before political consultants or campaign managers or even her father.

That victory was incredibly short-lived because she realized a call from a campaign manager could only mean one thing. One terrible, awful thing.

"Your father is going to be running for the US Senate seat in the state of Missouri—were you aware that it recently became open?"

Christine did not throw up all over her desk. Score one for adulting. "I was not."

"Sex scandals are such a tricky thing to negotiate. And the people of Missouri are going to be looking for someone with an unimpeachable character and record—someone like your father."

Maybe she was so tired that she had fallen asleep at her desk and was having a nightmare. *Wake up*, she told herself.

Brian White kept talking. "What we'd like to do is make you a part of this campaign. A redemption story, if you will."

Oh, God. "No, I don't think I will."

Because she had a very good idea of what a redemption story would look like to her father. There would be a public confession of her many, many sins. Probably something resembling a walk of shame. And that was just for starters. Her father would expect her to go on talk shows and accompany him on the campaign trail. Knowing him, he would expect her to find a nice man and then make Marie legitimate by getting married.

Her heart was going to beat itself right out of her chest. She had to physically hold on to the desk to keep from falling out of her chair when Mr. White said, "Oh, I think you will. You're a very important part of your father's campaign and he insists on bringing you back into the fold."

She hadn't heard from the man since his last concession speech—a garbled screed against sin and the devil where he had apologized to his faithful believers for his daughter, who had stained his quest for truth, justice and the American way. "He's had almost two years to bring me back in the fold and he can't even bring himself to do it. He has to get his lapdog to call me."

White chuckled. "I can see this is a bad time. I'll call again in a couple of days, when you've had time to think the proposition over. You are going to want my help, Ms. Murray. Because without it…"

It wasn't so much a threat as a statement of fact. She was about to lose control of her life all over again and for what? For her father's misguided attempts at winning a political office?

Last time had been bad enough. Her every misdeed, her every bad picture—all that had suddenly become fodder for the gossip mill. The television commercials had been the worst—her photos had been distorted so she looked like a stupid cow chewing cud instead of a woman who was six months pregnant. It had been the darkest time of her life.

This time would be so much worse because they wouldn't just come for her. She had survived that kind of attack once before. It was awful and painful, but she had survived.

No, this time they would come for Marie. Her precious little girl.

Christine hung up the phone and somehow made it to the ladies' room. She locked herself in a stall and sobbed. Why was her father doing this? Why was he doing it to *her*? She knew Clarence Murray didn't love her. But surely he had a little human decency—just enough that he would want to shield his only granddaughter from the media?

Oh, who was she kidding? Her father had never considered anyone else's needs. The only thing that mattered was what he decided God had meant for him to do.

"Christine? Are you okay?"

It was Sue, a teller who was Christine's best work friend. How long had she been in there? She dried her eyes on industrial-grade toilet paper and opened the door. "I'm fine."

But even as she said it, Sue gasped and recoiled in horror before throwing her arms around Christine's shoulders and hugging her. "Oh, honey—who died?"

Christine almost laughed because if she didn't, she would start crying again. "It's nothing."

The ramifications of her father's latest campaign began to spin out for her. The bank's owner, Mr. Whalen, would not appreciate this sort of attention. She might have to uproot her life. Go somewhere new and start over.

The prospect was daunting. With what money? She had a couple hundred socked away in the bank, which was not a heck of a lot. She didn't want to have to give up her life, her identity—to say nothing of her privacy and sanity— just so her father could lose a campaign again.

What was she going to do?

One of the reasons she had moved to Denver was that fewer people knew who she was. Murray was just another last name here.

So Christine did what she had to do—she lied again. "I'm hormonal and Marie is teething and I'm *so* tired." Not that it was much of a lie. She merely left out the bits about political intrigue.

"Here, let me fix you up." Sue produced her purse, which was sixty-three percent makeup. Christine felt a moment of longing for those days. Currently, her purse consisted of diapers, wet wipes, bibs, crayon stubs, random Cheerios and things she didn't want to think about. Glamour and beauty were low on her list right now.

Still, there was something comforting about letting Sue apply under-eye concealer and powder her face, especially since Sue was relatively close in coloring to Christine and was only a few inches shorter—they'd been able to swap clothes a few times.

"Am I in trouble, do you think?" She had no idea how long she had been hiding in the ladies' room. All she knew was that Brian White and Clarence Murray and the media couldn't reach her in there. If she did not have to pick up Marie tonight from day care, she would never leave the ladies' room. This place was her sanctuary.

Except for the small detail that she was still at work. "There's some guy out there waiting to talk to you." Christine must have looked stricken because Sue quickly added, "He's not mad or anything. He's *hot*. Tall, dark—extremely handsome. I didn't see a ring."

It was all she could do to get her mouth closed. "You checked him out?" But even as she said that, she felt the weight on her shoulders lighten ever so slightly. After Brian White had ruined her life, she'd looked him up on the internet. He was not tall. He was not dark. No one would ever accuse him of being handsome. The man was short, pudgy and balding.

Which meant that whoever was waiting for her at her desk was not a campaign manager representing her father.

"Of course," Sue said. "Wait until you see him. I bet he's a male model. Maybe even a movie star—he's that *hot*."

Christine snorted. She didn't need hot—she needed help. Real, tangible help. She needed someone who would get Brian White and her father to leave her alone. She needed someone who could help her protect Marie. She needed brains and brawn. And she needed enough money to pay for all of that.

She might as well ask for a unicorn for her birthday. "We don't give out loans based on hotness."

"We should. There," Sue added. "You look human again."

Christine hugged her friend and strengthened her mental resolve. "Thank you. I better get out there and meet Mr. Hot."

If she couldn't get through one day at a time, she'd take it one hour at a time. One minute at a time.

Sixty seconds. She could do this.

God, she hoped.

Two

Her courage fortified and her under-eye bags hidden, Christine headed to her desk. She rounded the corner and pulled up short—Sue had not been lying. The gentleman waiting for her was *beyond* hot. His dark hair was perfectly slicked back, giving him a smooth look. And was that suit custom-made?

Even though he was casually sitting in the chair in front of her desk, one leg crossed over the other, she got the impression of a knife—sharp and potentially dangerous. When he noticed her, he came to his feet like a cat uncoiling from a nap. She revised her earlier opinion. He was not potentially dangerous—he *was* dangerous.

"Ms. Murray." There was a tone of the familiar in his voice and she felt herself gritting her teeth. Did he know who she was?

"Welcome to the First City Bank of Denver." Because she was at work, she extended her hand in a polite businessperson's handshake. "And you are?"

He stared down at her for a moment and she almost got lost in his light brown eyes. Up close, she realized that his hair wasn't black—there was a hint of red that lightened the color to a deep mahogany. It was a striking look on the man.

Against her will, her pulse began to flutter in her neck. Men generally did not look at her with interest. She was short and chunky and she couldn't be one hundred percent sure she didn't have oatmeal stains from Marie's breakfast on her shirt.

"Lee." He slid his hand into hers but instead of the acceptable three-pump handshake, he just held her hand, palm to palm. "Daniel Lee." As he said his name—slowly and carefully—he studied her.

What was this? Was he checking to see what her reaction would be?

She swallowed nervously. Was she supposed to know who he was? Something about him seemed familiar. Maybe he was a movie star? Or at least a cable TV star? But his name didn't ring a bell. He was so incredibly gorgeous that it was making it hard for her to think.

She should have stayed in the ladies' room. "How can I help you today, Mr. Lee?" she said, taking sanctuary behind her desk. She felt better with four feet of wood between them.

He stood for a moment too long, staring down at her. Nervously, she lifted her gaze back to him. The suit was most definitely custom-made—the shirt was, also. Those trappings did little to disguise the raw power of his body. Again, she thought of a dagger in a perfectly made sheath. He was the sort of man who always got his way.

The sort she avoided like the plague. Because men like him never cared for women like her and they certainly never cared for babies like Marie. Christine was tired of being collateral damage.

She motioned toward the chair. She couldn't handle him looming over her.

He sat, somehow making her standard-issue office chair look as regal as a throne. "I don't think the question is what you can do for me, Ms. Murray. The question is what I can do for you."

She needed to start carrying pepper spray. "I'm not interested."

One corner of his mouth—not that she was staring—curved into a deadly smile. Christine was both simultaneously thankful that Sue had fixed her face and upset that she had. If only Christine looked like she was having the worst day of her life, this man might not be staring at her quite so intently. "Are you sure? You don't even know why I'm here."

This was something that was different from two years ago. Then, when the reporters had first started showing up at her home and following her to work in Kansas City, she hadn't been ready for it. Footage of her stammering and looking petrified was all over the internet. Even she had to admit that she looked guilty as sin in those videos.

But she learned how to brace herself for the attacks and how to keep her face relatively calm. She wasn't the same clueless girl she'd been back then. And besides, she already had advance warning.

"Who sent you? My father?"

That dangerous smile fell away from his face. *Ha*, Christine thought. She'd caught him off guard and that counted for something.

"No. But I'm going to make an educated guess that you received a phone call today—probably from Brian White." Although she didn't want to react, she could feel the blood draining out of her face. This guy knew who Brian White was? "Yes," he said in a voice that might have been gentle coming from anyone else. "I can see that you did. I was hoping to get to you before he did."

"Who do you work for?" And as much as she wanted to sound strong and brave, her voice came out shaky. Because how much did one woman have to endure?

Something flashed over his eyes and if she didn't know better, she would've said it was guilt. "I am the executive vice-president and chief marketing officer of the Beaumont Brewery. I do not work for your father, nor do I work for any potential opponents of his. I have no interest in forcing you to publicly…" He waved a hand, as if he could pull the right words out of thin air. "Repudiate your life choices, nor do I have any interest in using them against you."

Well. At least he hadn't called Marie a sin. Although "life choice" wasn't a huge step up.

Wait. Was that why he looked familiar? He was one of those bastards—Beaumont's bastards. His brother or half brother—she had no hope of ever keeping the Beaumonts straight—had taken over the brewery. She'd only been in Denver for a few months when that happened. And besides, she didn't drink anymore.

Why was the executive vice-president of the Beaumont Brewery offering her help? It felt like a trap. A really obvious trap. "Who are you, really?"

He didn't answer the question. "I know what's coming— and so do you. Because here's what happened. Mr. White offered to redeem your reputation and, when you refused his so-called help, he threatened to make an example of you."

Her vision swam. She wanted to go someplace quiet and dark and lie down and close her eyes and open them again and find out this entire thing had been one never-ending nightmare.

But this Daniel Lee was right. "How do you know?"

He looked pained—truly pained. He stood and pulled out a business card. He extended it to her, but she didn't take it from him and, after an awkward moment, he set it on the corner of her desk. "Because I was the one who found out you were pregnant. I'm the one who made it a news story. Everything that happened to you was a direct result of my actions, which means that—" he went on, ignoring Christine's gasp of horror "—everything that happens to you from this point on is also my responsibility. You're going to get dragged, Christine. I know what White is capable of and we both know what your father is capable of. You need my help. You can't handle this by yourself."

"Get out." She wanted to stand to make her point, but she didn't trust her legs. It was *him*. This slick, smooth, unfortunately hot man had helped Brian White ruin her life. She really was going to throw up, adulting be damned. "If I see you anywhere near me or my daughter, I'm calling the police."

He inclined his head in her direction, something that was almost a bow. "As you wish. But the offer stands. I no longer work as a political consultant, but I know how to play the game. I can protect you. You and your daughter." He touched the tip of his index finger to the top of the silver frame that held a small picture of Marie on her first birthday.

Christine's mouth was dry and her throat wasn't working. She desperately wanted to tell this man to go to hell but before she could form the words, he gave her another one of those half bows, turned on his heel, and walked away.

* * *

Christine began to search during her breaks. Although
he had not officially declared his candidacy, "sources close
to Clarence Murray" were leaking teasers about his up-
coming campaign—the kind of leaks that were designed to
inspire his political base and raise funds from the faithful.

She couldn't find *anything* about Daniel Lee. She didn't
even bother looking for Brian White. White was the scum
of the earth and she didn't want him to pollute her brain
any more than necessary.

But Lee confused her. He had taken full credit for dragging her into the last campaign. If—and it was a huge *if*—
his offer of help had been sincere, it had almost been…
an apology.

But she couldn't even find a mention of him that existed before he suddenly appeared by Zeb Richards's side
at the Beaumont Brewery. His official brewery biography
stated that he had a long history of working for political
campaigns but the man was like a ghost. And with a last
name like Lee, there was no way to track him down.

She found herself staring at his official company photo.
It wasn't fair how good-looking he was. If she had to guess,
she would say he was at least part Asian—but that didn't
exactly narrow things down. Lee was a popular name in
several Asian countries. Searching "Daniel Lee" led to an
overwhelming number of results.

She didn't want his help. Frankly, she didn't want anyone's help. If there was one thing she had learned, it was
that relying on other people was asking to be disappointed.
She had thought she could rely on Doyle. After all, they'd
been engaged. They'd taken the first step in publicly de-
claring their love. They'd created a child together.

But when she'd really needed him, Doyle had run. Not
that she could blame him—if she could have gotten away

from the media attention, she would've. Still, it hurt. It hurt that he sent a monthly child support check and had nothing to do with his daughter.

It was foolish to keep hoping that no one would pay attention to Christine and her daughter. But short of calling Daniel Lee and asking what, exactly, he had in mind when he said he could protect her and Marie, she didn't know what else to do.

So she did nothing. She did her job and she took care of her daughter and foolishly hoped for the best.

"Who's the target?"

Daniel leveled a look at Porter Cole, the private investigator who'd done work for him in Denver on numerous occasions. Referring to Christine as a "target" grated on Daniel's nerves. "Christine Murray."

Porter made it his job to know things. "What are we looking for?"

Porter had done more than enough work for Daniel to trust him with sensitive directives. But Daniel wasn't about to let the man know he had suddenly developed a conscience. "You're not looking for anything about her."

Porter stared at him in confusion. "Then what are we doing?"

"I have reason to believe she's about to get a tail. I want to know who's watching her and her daughter, when and for how long. And I want the means to get them off her tail. Outstanding warrants, whatever it takes."

Seeing Christine Murray in person had made everything a thousand times worse. Had he thought she was beautiful before? In person, she was so much more than that. Delicate and vulnerable—scared and mad—but underneath was a core of strength that took everything lovely about her and made her that much more attractive.

Porter notched an eyebrow as he scanned the file on Christine. "Any particular reason?"

"None that you need to know." Which was a bit of posturing and Daniel knew it. Porter was a smart man, more than capable of connecting the dots. "As usual, do not engage unless there's a threat."

"Contact for defense only. Got it. Anything else?" He handed the file back to Daniel.

"No." Daniel took the file and put it in his desk drawer, which he then locked. "Absolute secrecy, as always."

"As always." Porter gave him a long look before standing and straightening his blazer, which concealed his gun. "If you don't mind me saying, I thought you got out of politics."

"I did. This isn't politics."

Porter smirked as he walked out of Daniel's office and said, "You'll be hearing from me," as if he didn't believe Daniel.

For once, it was the unvarnished truth.

What he was doing for Christine Murray—it wasn't politics.

It was personal.

Daniel waited impatiently. Normally, waiting was something he did well. He played a long game—always had. It was one of the things he'd learned at his grandfather's knee back in Seoul, South Korea. Most people looked at the trees. A few people could stand in front of the trees and know they were looking at the forest. But they wouldn't have any idea of how big that forest was. Daniel prided himself on knowing every tree in every acre in the never-ending forest.

He had Christine Murray figured for one of two things. One, she would either call him in a state of blind panic the moment her face appeared on the internet again. Or two, she would disappear.

Okay, maybe that was overstating. Because even though she had clearly been upset when he had approached her at work, she hadn't panicked. She'd maintained her composure and even gotten in a couple of good digs at him.

He couldn't help it. He admired her. It felt risky, this admiration. Combined with the attraction he couldn't quite rein in, it made Christine Murray feel dangerous. She made him want to do things that weren't logical.

Things like pay for private investigators to shadow her. He'd already gotten a report from Porter Cole. Porter had caught a guy trying to break into Christine's apartment while she was at work. According to his report, Porter had acted like he was a resident of the apartment complex and scared the guy off. But both Daniel and Porter knew that wouldn't be the end of it. Someone wanted inside Christine's apartment, no doubt to gather evidence that could be used against her in the court of public opinion.

Porter said there was also a woman who lingered near the child's day care. At pick up and drop off, and when the children went out to the playground, the woman was within line of sight. Probably taking pictures of the little girl Daniel had seen in the small frame on Christine's desk.

The little girl had wispy light brown hair, but her eyes were almost exactly like her mother's brilliant blue ones. Except innocent and hopeful, instead of trapped and scared.

Christine didn't want his help but she desperately needed it. It would be so much easier if she were willing to talk to him. They could coordinate and come up with a plan that would minimize this disruption to her and her daughter's lives.

But that wasn't going to happen. At least not immediately. Daniel revised his original opinion. She would not call him in a panic the moment she became an internet story. She'd already told Brian off and then told him off. She wouldn't be spooked by a little media coverage. She'd try to brazen it out just like she had at the bank. It was a brave choice. Stupid, but brave.

No, Daniel wouldn't hear from Christine when she became news. But when her daughter became news?

That was when she would either call him or disappear.

He figured he had a week before Clarence Murray announced his candidacy for the open US Senate seat in Missouri.

If only his grandfather could see him now. Lee Dae-Won wouldn't contain his disappointment at Daniel's choices—yet again. Daniel had never been smart enough or ambitious enough or legitimate enough—and certainly never Korean enough—for his grandfather. All might have been forgiven if Daniel had married any of the dozens of acceptable Korean women his grandfather had paraded in front of him over the years and started a family to carry on the family business.

Daniel had steadfastly refused to marry anyone, much less father any children. And he had refused to move to South Korea permanently and live under his grandfather's thumb. It had driven the old man insane that his only heir had rejected the family business, Lee Enterprises.

Daniel liked to think that, at least as a political consultant, he had made the old man proud. Lee Dae-Won hadn't become one of the richest men in South Korea by investing wisely in real estate and electronic manufacturing. Daniel's grandfather had gained power through manipulation, lies and outright bribery. He had trafficked in secrets and that, more than family honor or loyalty, was what Daniel had learned at his knee during summer vacations spent at the family compound in Seoul.

He who controlled the information controlled the world.

Daniel hated not being in control.

He shouldn't care about what happened to Christine or her daughter. At the very least, the basic security measures he was enacting on her behalf should relieve him of his guilt.

It didn't.

Because he had to admit that he did care. He'd catch himself staring at her photo again. And that? That had nothing to do with guilt.

He hoped she'd call him. That was all he could do. The next contact had to be hers.

That didn't mean there wasn't anything else he could be doing right now, though. He scrolled through his contacts list until he found the number he was looking for.

"Hello, Daniel," Natalie Wesley said, answering on the second ring. "Is this a business call or not?"

"What's to say it's not both?" he asked, trying to sound like he was teasing her and knowing he was failing miserably. "How are you and CJ?"

CJ Wesley was another one of Daniel's half brothers—another one of Hardwick Beaumont's bastards. CJ was the one who hadn't wanted anything to do with the Beaumont Brewery. He was a rancher up on the northeast side of Denver and he preferred his privacy. Which made it all the funnier that he had married the former television personality Natalie Baker—the same woman who had tried to expose his parentage to the world.

Natalie was one of the very few people who had been able to locate CJ and ascertain his identity. Plus, she'd had her own morning news show, *A Good Morning With Natalie Baker*, for almost a decade. She was an investigative

journalist who knew how to talk to the cameras. "We're
fine. You should come up and see us. CJ is determined to
get you on a horse, you know."

"I'll do that sometime," Daniel said. While of course
he cared for CJ—he was fond of nearly all of his half
siblings—CJ was the hardest to be around. His mother
had married a good man and he'd had a good life. CJ was
at ease with himself in a way that Daniel could never
pull off. "I have a situation that I'm going to need your
help with."

Natalie sighed. "The offer stands, Daniel. But what
is it?"

"What do you know about Christine Murray?"

"Who?"

So, over the next twenty minutes, Daniel filled her in.
"Thus far, she hasn't accepted my help. But when she does,
we'll need to do damage control."

"Manipulate the search rankings, plant positive news
articles, maybe an interview?"

"Yes."

"Got it." There was a pause and Daniel braced for the
sisterly concern. "We worry about you, you know."

"Why?" His health was great. He was helping to run
the third-largest brewery in America and he owned a
substantial share of Lee Enterprises. He owned homes
in Seoul, Denver and Chicago. What was there to worry
about?

Okay, so he was a little troubled about Christine Murray and her daughter. But that wasn't cause for alarm.

"Daniel…" Her voice trailed off. "Never mind. I'll look
into this and get back to you if I find out anything."

It was strange that he felt disappointed she hadn't said
something else. Even though he had no idea what he
wanted her to say. "Thanks." He ended the call and re-

freshed the tab he kept open with his searches on Christine Murray. There was nothing new. Not yet, anyway.

But there would be. Soon.

Three

Everything, it seemed, happened at once. One moment, Christine was just doing her job at the bank and trying not to think about the worst-case scenarios *or* Daniel Lee and his seemingly sincere offer of help. Or the way he filled out a suit.

Suddenly, the alerts she had set up on web searches started piling up in her inbox. Clarence Murray had declared his candidacy for the open US Senate seat. Her phone started to ring, as if people had just been waiting for the official announcement. She was trying to read the article about her father and trying to answer the phone in her business-professional voice and saying no comment over and over again when *it* happened.

Will Murray's Granddaughter Cost Him This Election, Too?

And there it was—the photo of her with Marie on her hip, alongside her Honda Civic. It wasn't a good photo—

clearly, it had been taken from some distance. The image was so grainy it could have been almost anyone.

But it was her daughter. They knew where she was and they knew how to take pictures of her daughter and suddenly, Christine couldn't bear it.

With hands shaking, she pulled the nondescript business card out from underneath her office phone. She had wanted to throw Daniel Lee's card away—but she'd been unable to do it. Because what he'd said had felt true, somehow.

Would he actually help her? Or was he working an angle that she hadn't found yet?

Her phone rang again and this time, she recognized the voice on the other end. Brian White—the devil she didn't want to know. "Ms. Murray," he said, as if they were the oldest of friends. "I'm checking back in with you. As you may have heard, your father has officially declared his candidacy and I—"

She hung up the phone. She didn't want to hear his fake offers of help and she especially did not want to hear his thinly veiled threats.

She did the only thing she could—she grabbed her cell phone and hurried to the ladies' room. Daniel Lee's card was a plain white rectangle of paper with two lines of text set directly in the middle—his name and a telephone number. She was shaking so violently that she misdialed the number twice before she finally got it right and even then, she sat for a moment on the stool in the farthest stall and wondered if she wasn't about to make the biggest mistake of her life.

But then she thought about the headline, the one implying that a fourteen-month-old baby had the power to decide elections. The photos would only get better and the headlines would only get worse.

She hit the button and held the phone to her ear. "This is Daniel."

"Um, hello. You gave me your card—"

"Christine? Are you all right?"

She forced herself to take a deep breath and tried to swallow around the lump in her throat. No, she was not all right. Not even close. "Hi. Um, I need to know if what you said when you talked to me last week still applies. The offer about, um, helping me and my daughter?"

"You saw the articles?"

Her vision began to swim and she couldn't tell if she was about to pass out or if she was just crying again. "There's more than one?"

There was a long pause. "That's not important right now. What is important is that you make sure you and your daughter are safe and that we can get together and formulate a plan."

It sounded good. Someone was concerned with their safety. Someone had a plan and the means of enacting it. If life were perfect, this would be the answer to her prayers.

Life had never been perfect. "How do I know I can trust you? How do I know you didn't write those articles or take those pictures? How do I know you're not setting me up?"

"You don't."

Well, if that didn't just beat all. She let out a frustrated laugh. "You're not inspiring confidence right now."

"I'm being honest. You and I both know that if I told you I had nothing to do with those articles and promised you that you could trust me, it would only make you doubt me even more."

Darn it, he was right. But the heck of it was, she didn't have much of a choice right now. Her options were few and far between and there was no guarantee that when she went to pick up Marie after work today there wouldn't be a pack of people with cameras waiting for them. "Fine. But I don't have to like it."

"If you liked it, we wouldn't be having this conversation. Instead, you'd be holding an impromptu press conference in the bank's parking lot. We need to meet, Christine."

Her stomach turned. She leaned forward, putting her head between her knees. "I don't want you in my home. Don't take it personally."

"I don't. Besides, I'm not going to your apartment. One of the worst things that could happen would be for a strange man to be photographed entering and leaving your apartment. Similarly, you can't come to my place. If you're followed—and I think it's safe to assume you will be— that's another set of headlines that neither of us wants."

Okay, so he was being honest. "You want to meet in public?" Because that also seemed like a bad idea.

"And risk more media coverage? Out of the question."

She honestly didn't know if this conversation was making her feel better or worse. "So if we can't meet in private and we can't meet in public, how the heck are we supposed to meet?"

"You attend the Red Rock church, correct?"

She squeezed her eyes shut. "I suppose I shouldn't be surprised you know that."

Red Rock was her attempt to bridge the evangelical teachings of her childhood with the faith that was in her heart. She needed a spiritual home and a nondenominational megachurch was a good place to disappear.

Plus, they had a nice child care center. Going to Sunday services was as close as she got to a weekly break.

"Which service do you normally attend—the nine a.m. or the ten forty-five?"

"The later one," This seemed like a bad idea. Meeting

with a—well, she didn't really know what to call Daniel Lee. He certainly wasn't a friend. Maybe a spy? Finally, she decided on *associate*. Meeting an associate like Daniel Lee in church seemed colossally wrong.

But sometimes, there simply was no right option.

"Which side of the chapel do you sit on?"

"I'm surprised you don't know," she snapped. Immediately, she added, "Sorry. I'm under a lot of stress right now."

"There's no need to apologize. If I know which side you sit on, it'll make it easier to find you. I don't want it to look like you're looking for me. I would like you to think if there is a classroom or a small alcove—an out-of-the-way place where we could chat without being conspicuous about it. Can you do that?"

"There will be people around. Over two thousand people go to this church."

"We're not hiding. We're merely being inconspicuous."

Was she supposed to understand that distinction? "I sit on the far left side. It's close to the aisle and closer to the child care center if there's a problem. And there are a few places where we could talk with minimal interruptions." She hoped.

Actually, the idea of meeting in a semipublic place like the church wasn't half-bad. She didn't want to be alone with him. But if they were in the church, there would be people around. It was probably as safe as it was going to get.

"Excellent. I'll find you after the service. But don't hesitate to call me before then if there's something you need help with."

"All right." It was Friday. Surely, she could make it through a day and a half, right?

"Christine, I'm serious. If you see someone around who

makes you uncomfortable, try to get a picture of them, then call me immediately."

"What are you going to do that the police couldn't?"

There was another pause, one that felt heavy and ominous. "I'll see you on Sunday," he said, completely avoiding the question. "Keep a low profile until then."

That made her laugh even as her eyes began to water again. "I've been doing that for the last year and a half. I go to work, I go grocery shopping and I go home. I do my laundry and then take care of my daughter. I don't have wild nights on the town. I don't take lovers. I'm the most boring person I know and see what good it's done me?" She only realized she was shouting because her voice echoed off the tiled walls of the bathroom. "It doesn't matter how low my profile is. I'm nothing but bait in a sea of sharks. And it's all your fault."

She didn't know what she expected him to do. Defend himself? Yell? Point out that, if she had managed to get married before she'd gotten pregnant, none of this would have happened? That was her father's favorite. This was nobody's fault but her own.

Daniel Lee said none of those things. "I know. Just remember that help is a phone call away. You're not alone." And just like that, he ended the call, leaving her in a state of shock.

Had he just admitted that she was right? That didn't seem possible. Someone as gorgeous and refined as Daniel Lee—he wasn't the kind of person who owned up to his mistakes—was he?

As tempting as it was, she knew she could not hide out in the ladies' room for the rest of her workday. Sooner or later, her bosses would send Sue to find her and then there would be another makeover session and she would have to go back to her desk and stare at the voicemail, which by now was probably approaching hundreds of messages.

But she couldn't move just yet. She didn't trust that man. She wasn't entirely sure she trusted anyone.

You're not alone.

Oh, if only that were true.

One of the many things Daniel had learned at a young age was how to blend in. Going to school in Chicago had been easy. He had been surrounded by children of Korean descent and other Asians, Eastern Europeans and Africans, in addition to Americans of all colors. Americans could look like anyone and *be* like anyone.

It hadn't been that way in Seoul. Even as a child, he had stuck out. By the age of ten, he'd been taller than his mother and by the age of twelve, taller than his grandfather. His hair and eyes weren't black. His eyes would never be as green as his half brother Zeb's, but they were a light brown and his hair had an almost reddish look to it.

Most Americans guessed he was Asian, but Koreans knew he was American on sight.

So he had learned how to blend in. His grandfather had paid for a private tutor to instruct him on Korean social manners and Daniel had been an eager student—first, in the hope that he would fit into his grandfather's world and then, when it became apparent he never would, just to show up the old man. Similarly, every fall when he came back to Chicago after three long months in Seoul, he had to relearn how to shake hands, how to tell American jokes—hell, even how to walk. He took longer strides in Chicago.

He was good at blending, though. Sometimes, due to his coloring, people thought he might be Hispanic. Daniel had learned not to mind. People saw what they wanted to see, which made it easier to blend in.

Take this Sunday morning, for instance. People wanted to see a potential new church member and Daniel gave them what they wanted. He was wearing a pair of brown corduroys and a thick cable knit sweater over a denim shirt. On top of all of that, he had on a ski jacket and snow boots and a knit cap pulled over his ears. He'd added a pair of glasses. In other words, he looked nothing like Daniel Lee but everything like a hipster attendee of a megachurch.

Daniel wanted to see Christine with his own eyes. He was responsible for dragging her name through the mud—that wasn't even a question. But what if...

What if she was just as crazy as her father was? What if she was a manipulative, coldhearted woman?

He didn't think so. When he had dug up all that dirt on her two years ago, he hadn't found anyone who'd described her that way. She'd gone through a wild phase in high school, but lots of teenagers rebelled. Besides, Christine had settled down in college. She'd met the man who'd fathered her daughter and gotten her life together.

Until Daniel had blown it up.

It was easy to get lost in a crowd of this size. The day was cold and everyone was bundled up. Aside from his clothing, all he needed was a friendly smile and a certain eagerness in his gaze.

He let the crowd carry him into the lobby. He snagged a program and pretended to read it as he studied the crowd. He didn't see anyone out of the ordinary, but then again, whoever was shadowing Christine was probably trying to blend in just as much as he was.

And then she walked right past him, that little girl in her arms. Marie, he mentally corrected himself. She wasn't just a little girl. She was the child Christine would do anything to protect.

Christine didn't notice him. She was busy chatting with

her daughter, getting her puffy pink coat unzipped and the stocking cap off her head. It was the first time he'd seen Christine smile. God, she was stunning when she was happy.

Marie had a red nose and redder cheeks, but a big smile that she spread around the room. She even looked at Daniel and grinned, her blue eyes lighting up as if she had been waiting for him all this time.

It felt like someone had punched him in the chest. Marie really did have Christine's eyes, hopeful and happy. And it seemed like Marie's little face answered at least some of Daniel's questions.

Then they were gone, disappearing down a long hall-way with a steady stream of parents jostling other small children. The crowd began to move into the auditorium and Daniel moved with them, trying to stick to the back. He didn't see either of the people Porter had identified as watching Christine, which was good.

Daniel had grown up going to a church where the ser-vice was performed in Korean in Chicago, but he was not deeply religious. He knew too much about people in power, which included religious leaders.

Nonetheless, it felt awkward to be spying on the woman in the house of God and even more wrong to be looking for other spies. He wanted at least one place to be a sanc-tuary for Christine.

She was one of the last people to come back into the auditorium as the band started up. This was the kind of church that had a rock 'n' roll band in addition to gospel singing and hymns. It had a little bit of everything, with high definition video presentations and surround-sound audio.

He watched Christine without staring at her. As she settled into her seat, she nodded and smiled and said a few things to the people around her. People treated her as they would any good acquaintance they saw once a week—they were friendly, but not overly warm. Which was good. He wasn't sure how far that first story had gotten. Christine as a news item hadn't been picked up by network television yet. Wonky political sites didn't have much reach outside of the political set. Plus, they were in Colorado, not Missouri.

The service was a solid hour and a half of preaching and singing and clapping. It was an engaging service, but Daniel wasn't really paying attention. He was mentally running through all the potential outcomes.

Natalie had already started flooding the internet with positive mentions of Christine. Even if Christine wasn't actually discussed in the article, Natalie was referencing her in the title to drive down search engine results on the other news articles. More official press releases would be released on Monday and Tuesday.

As tempting as it would be to think that would be that, Daniel knew better. Christine and her daughter were too tempting a target, the political writ large on something that should've been personal. The primary voting for the special election was a mere two months away and, God forbid Murray actually get his party's nomination, the election was only two months after that. A lot could happen in four months.

The service ended with a thundering song that brought everyone to their feet and they stayed there, chatting with friends as the crowd thinned. Other parents made a beeline for the direction of the day care—but not Christine. She leaned on a pew, smiling at the person who'd been sitting in front of her—but Daniel noticed the way she was surreptitiously glancing around the room. Looking for him.

Suddenly, he was gripped with a strange urge to make

her *see* him. He wanted her to look at him and recognize him and—he knew it was completely unreasonable—he wanted her to be happy to see him.

He had no business wanting such a thing. Obviously, what he really wanted was to be absolved of any guilt he had about the situation she now found herself in.

And then it almost happened. She *did* notice him. Her eyes grew wide with recognition. But it wasn't with happiness. At best, he would call her expression one of grim acceptance.

He deserved nothing more.

He gently inclined his head to the left, gesturing toward the hallway. Her chin moved down ever so slightly.

Daniel headed into the hall, which was bustling with parents trying to get their children back into winter gear and children refusing to be coddled. The hallway was almost as loud as the band had been—and that was saying something. Another few minutes passed before Christine appeared. Daniel did not follow her. He focused on looking lost and overwhelmed. In all this noise, it wasn't hard.

By the time Christine and Marie reappeared, many families had left and it was starting to quiet down. Christine was tickling the little girl's tummy and Marie was shrieking with joy. Unexpectedly, Daniel felt an overwhelming urge to protect her. Marie was completely innocent and for the time being, anyway, he was glad Christine had called him.

She was looking for him this time. Her gaze met his and the lines around her mouth tightened. It was not a reaction he enjoyed inspiring in people.

That wasn't entirely true. When he was looking at an opponent, the little sign of displeasure would be a good thing. But it bothered him coming from her.

She said loudly, "Sweetie, I think we left your hat in the day care," before turning around.

Daniel followed at a safe distance. No one else did. The day care was downstairs and, outside of the room, there was a grouping of chairs and a sofa, along with some toys and books on a beat-up coffee table. It looked like someone had donated a living room and the church had stuck the whole set in a glorified hallway, but it was quiet and no one else came in or out of the day care.

Christine settled onto the couch and clutched Marie as if she were afraid to let her go. "I wasn't sure if you would actually come."

"I gave you my word."

Her brow wrinkled. An irrational need to wipe away the doubt hit him. He wanted to make her smile, like he'd seen before the service. He wanted that smile all for himself.

He wasn't going to get it. "You'll forgive me if that doesn't mean a lot to me at this point."

She still had a lot of fight in her. A grin tugged at his lips, which made her eyes widen. "Understood, but when I make a promise to you, I'm going to keep that promise."

He hadn't always operated like that. But he had turned over a new leaf when he had accepted his role in the Beaumont Brewery and the Beaumont family. He did not lie to his relatives. And he wouldn't lie to Christine.

She gave him a long look, as if she were debating whether or not to believe this particular statement. "So, what do we do now?" But the words had barely left her mouth when Marie squirmed off her lap. Christine set her down and the little girl began to sidestep her way around the coffee table.

"I have a few questions and a couple of suggestions. And then we'll come up with a plan that minimizes the disruption to your life and keeps Marie as safe as possible."

She took a deep breath and let it out slowly before nodding her head. "All right. Although I can't imagine there's something about me you don't know. Not if you're the one who found out about her first."

He felt a pang of regret—but at the same time, he was encouraged. That backbone of steel gave a flinty edge to Christine's vulnerability and damned if he didn't like it.

No, no—not like. *Appreciate.* He appreciated her resolve. "Again, let me apologize for that."

She tried to shrug, as if his destroying her life had been just another day. "All's fair in love and politics."

"No, it's not." She looked up at him sharply, but he went on, "How much contact do you have with Marie's father?"

She winced. "I don't. Every now and then, I'll send him a picture, but he doesn't even reply to those anymore. He pays child support on time, though—my father made sure of that. It's the only thing he's ever done for me."

"That's my next question," Daniel said, forcing himself to ignore the pain in her voice. He was trying to make it better. "How much contact do you have with your father?"

She shook her head. "He doesn't want to breathe the same air as me. He blames me for his last loss—even though he's lost so many elections. He's convinced himself that if it hadn't been for me, he would've won that one."

"You don't think he would have?"

She slumped in the chair. "Of course not. His world is black and white. He's right and everyone who doesn't agree with him is wrong. Most people can't live like that. I know I couldn't." She grimaced, something that was supposed to look like a smile and failed. "Needless to say, I was always wrong."

Her words made sense on a level Daniel didn't want to inspect too closely. "I don't think you're wrong, Christine."

Whatever attempt at a smile she had made faded. "It's

nice of you to say that but I still don't know why you're here or what you think you're going to get out of helping me."

"What I want isn't important. It's my responsibility to shield you and your daughter from the coming storm. That's all there is to it."

As he said it, he looked down at the little girl who was still cruising around the coffee table. As if she knew she was being talked about, she looked up at him and smiled a drooly smile. She made her way over to him and then, in a moment of bravery, let go of the coffee table and all but fell into his legs.

Acting on instinct, Daniel caught her. He had not dealt with children a great deal. He was an uncle several times over, thanks to all of his various half siblings. He had even held Zeb's daughter, Amanda. But that had been when the baby was asleep.

Marie was much larger, squirming and laughing as she looked up at him with those trusting blue eyes. "Hello, Marie."

Marie giggled in response to this and leaned in to him. She was warm and heavy and impossibly cute.

It felt like something shifted in his chest as he stared down at her, the past and future all mixed up in one innocent child.

Then she squirmed and pointed at the coffee table, leaning so far that he had to hold on to her to keep her from toppling over. "She wants to read you a book," Christine said, a note of caution in her voice.

"All right." He scooped one of the dog-eared books off the table. He flipped it open and the little girl began to make babbling sounds. She pointed at a picture and then looked up at him, her eyes so big and so blue. Then she paused.

"She's waiting for you to respond," Christine said. Daniel glanced up at her to see that she was watching this entire scene unfold with interest.

Respond? "Really?" he said, hoping that was what Marie wanted to hear.

It was, apparently. She turned the page and chattered before waiting for Daniel. So he said, "Really?" again, this time with more emphasis. Marie nodded, her downy hair floating around her head.

There was something awkward about this entire arrangement. He was sitting in the basement of a church that he did not attend, holding a child who was not his. But at the same time, there was something that felt…right about it, too. Marie was proof there could still be sweetness and innocence in the world.

That realization he'd had earlier hit him again, harder this time.

He had to protect her. He had to protect them both.

Four

Christine sat in utter confusion. She'd thought she was meeting with the slick, smooth-talking, dangerous man who had made vague promises about helping her weather the oncoming storm. But that's not what was happening.

When she'd seen him earlier, she'd almost jumped out of her skin. Gone was the executive vice-president of the Beaumont Brewery. And in his place was a man who was taking her breath away again and again. Seriously, if Sue had thought he was hot before, she would die of gorgeousness now.

Christine had no idea a cable-knit sweater could be so danged sexy. And the way he was cuddling her daughter? She'd say this was a dream come true but her dreams were never this good.

She shook her head. They had a limited amount of time before either Marie had a meltdown or someone noticed them and began to ask questions. She still had no idea if she could trust Daniel Lee, much less accept his help. She couldn't let her attraction to him muddy the waters, either. She was done being dependent on other people to protect her name or family.

So why couldn't she do anything but sit here and stare as Marie curled into his lap and read him a story as if her daughter had known him all of her young life?

And Daniel—the smooth, dangerous man who had showed up at Christine's work—he was playing along. He was turning the pages for Marie and saying "Really?" a lot—which was what Marie wanted. He wasn't checking his phone or his watch. He wasn't complaining about Marie's very existence.

He was the executive vice-president of the Beaumont Brewery. He was a political consultant who had screwed up her life.

He was a man holding her daughter as if he truly cared about her. A man who looked at her as if she were worth something.

Not even Doyle had held Marie like this. He had never come to see his own daughter. He hadn't replied to the last pictures Christine had sent from her first birthday. Marie was a persona non grata with both her father and her grandfather. They had never seen her as a person. She'd always been a chess piece, a pawn that they moved at will around the board for a game Christine didn't want to play.

And Daniel—he had been the one to start it all. Okay, that wasn't fair. She bore some of the responsibility. But she couldn't look at Marie and think of her perfect angel as a mistake.

"Really?" Daniel said again, cracking a huge smile when Marie drooled on him.

Christine was having trouble breathing. Daniel wasn't looking at Marie like she was a mistake or an accident. He was treating her as a perfectly normal fourteen-month-old baby. Was it wrong to want that?

No. It wasn't. It was the whole reason Christine was here with this man that she still did not trust.

Then Daniel leaned down and rested his cheek on the top of Marie's head. Christine saw him breathe deeply and she knew what he was smelling—Marie's sweet baby scent. Daniel sighed and in that moment, he looked so different from the man who had walked into the bank a week ago that she wouldn't have recognized him. He didn't look hard and sharp. He looked...

He looked perfect.

No. It was probably an act. She didn't believe he felt a responsibility for her and Marie. She absolutely could not let herself buy into whatever fiction he presented. She could not be seduced by tenderness *or* a chiseled jaw—or any combination of the two.

Marie finished the book and squirmed off his lap to go back to cruising around the table. Daniel watched her for a moment and then turned his eyes to Christine's. Heat flashed through her body, an awareness that she didn't want but couldn't seem to ignore. What was wrong with her?

"Where were we?"

Right. Yes. The point—that had nothing to do with the way her skin warmed under his gaze. "Neither my ex-fiancé nor my father has any contact with us."

A change came over his face. It didn't matter how cuddly he'd looked— he was still a weapon that could be used against her.

"And just so we're clear, do you have any interest in publicly reconciling with your father?"

"Why? He'll want me to repent, tell everyone I've seen the light and that his way is the one true way. He'll want me to go to campaign events and dress Marie as a little princess. He might even want me to get married—to someone he approves of, of course—so that Marie is no longer illegitimate." Christine shuddered at the thought of the man her father would approve of. "No. I'm not interested in being a bullet point in a fund-raising email or his mouthpiece and they *cannot* have my daughter."

He considered this statement for so long that she began to fidget. "It might shield you from some of the worst of it."

Was he seriously trying to talk her into this? "Let's say I go along with this insanity. I get an image makeover and follow my father's path. I marry someone who 'redeems' me. Then what? God forbid my father actually wins the election. Instead, he'll probably lose. Will he blame me for it again? Or—more likely—I'll break one of his rules. I *always* do, just by existing. Then what? Another public shaming? No."

Daniel was staring at her and she knew she needed a thicker skin. She knew that this was probably the most sympathetic audience she would get. But he was unnerving her anyway.

God, she was so tired of being judged. "You don't know what it's like," she went on bitterly, "never being good enough. Maybe if I'd been born a boy, it would've been different. But I can't change the fact that, in his eyes, I am marked by sin. You wouldn't understand."

And then she realized what she had just said—and who she had said it to. Maybe Daniel Lee, the political consultant, couldn't understand. But Daniel Lee, the illegitimate son of Hardwick Beaumont, might. "I'm sorry," she stammered. "I didn't mean…"

One corner of his mouth curved up. "It's perfectly fine. I do understand—I had a complicated relationship with my grandfather. I never knew my father." He said it so casually, as if being cut off from half of his heritage was no big deal.

Marie was going to grow up like that, too. She would never know Doyle or Doyle's family. They wanted nothing to do with either of them. Marie picked up on her distress and looked up, her lower lip quivering.

"I'm sorry," Christine repeated, smiling big to show her daughter that all was well. "That was rude of me. I... Well, I don't know anything about you and I think you know a lot about me and this is the most awkward thing ever, isn't it?"

He shrugged, somehow managing to look nonchalant and glamorous at the same time. He really was unfortunately hot. Hot and patient with small children and inexplicably offering to protect her. If circumstances weren't what they were, she could easily develop a huge crush on the man.

She'd always liked boys. *Always*. And the more her father had scolded her about her clothes, her attitude and especially her boyfriends, the more attractive boys had become.

Once, a lifetime ago, she'd started sneaking out of the house when she was fourteen. She'd been smoking by fifteen, drinking by then, too. And the boys...

But as she squirmed under Daniel's direct gaze, she realized that he was nothing like the boys she'd run wild with. He wasn't a boy in any sense of the word. Tall and lean, his hair that unusual mahogany color—so beautiful it was almost painful to look at him straight on—yeah, he was way hotter than any of the boys from her teen years.

But Daniel's appeal went way beyond his physical attributes. Because all of those guys she'd dated in high school and college—none of them would have stood by her side when the crap hit the fan. Doyle certainly hadn't—and

Doyle had been a pretty good guy. He'd paid his part of the bills and asked her to marry him and joked about her crazy dad with her. Sure, he hadn't made her wild with lust—but she'd always chalked that up to maturity. She'd gotten tired of fighting her father's dictates and she'd settled down.

What if it hadn't been maturity? What if it'd just been exhaustion?

Oh, it would be too easy to lust after this man. So she decided she wouldn't. "Look, Mr. Lee—"

He interrupted her. "Call me Daniel, Christine."

She didn't want to. It felt too intimate, to say his name like that. It was definitely too intimate to hear her name on his lips and intimacy was the last thing she needed if she was going to *not* lust after him.

She knew she was blushing and she was completely powerless to stop it. What she wouldn't give to face this man with cool indifference.

Then Marie piped up. "Daniel Tiger!" she said, looking up at Daniel with wild enthusiasm.

At least, that was what Marie meant. Christine had no trouble understanding her even if her pronunciation left something to be desired.

But that's not what Daniel heard. His eyes got wide as Marie banged on the top of the coffee table, warming to her theme and repeated *"anal grr!"* in a volume that was just short of a tornado siren.

"What did she say?" Daniel said, staring at Christine in shock. His cheeks had darkened as she got the distinct feeling he was trying not to laugh.

"Daniel Tiger. It's one of her favorite shows." When he blinked, she added, "He was a minor character on *Mr. Roger's Neighborhood*? They animated him and gave him his own show. She loves it."

"Daniel Tiger!" Marie screeched even louder. It still came out sounding like *"anal grr!"* though.

Daniel blinked a few more times, his eyes getting wider and wider. Then he hid his mouth behind his hand. "Kids say the darndest things?"

He was completely flustered, Christine realized. All it took was a fourteen-month-old with a lisp to knock him completely out of his groove. She allowed herself to smile as she wondered how many people got to see him like this. She was tempted to let Marie keep going—and she knew her daughter could—but time was of the essence.

"Honey," she said to Marie, "why don't you read me a story while Mr. Lee and I keep talking?"

For a moment, she thought her daughter would balk but then she spotted a *Pat the Bunny* book. She slid along the coffee table and cuddled into Christine's arms, ready to tell some long-winded story about a bunny that even Christine wouldn't be able to understand.

"Sorry for the interruptions. This is life with a toddler."

Daniel still had his mouth hidden behind his hand, but she could tell he was grinning wildly. "Not a problem. Although it would probably be best if we didn't let her say that near any microphones."

She wanted to laugh but the mention of microphones reminded her why she was here. "You don't think I'm a bad person for letting her watch television, do you? Or is that the sort of thing people will say makes me an unfit mother?"

The smile fell away from his eyes as his hand fell away from his mouth. "I'm sure there are a few sanctimonious idiots who'd make that case. But in reality, letting a young child watch an age-appropriate television show while you cook dinner or breakfast, I assume, is what most everyone does."

Marie looked up at her and Christine said, "Oh, really?" which was what Marie wanted to hear. She turned the page and kept on telling her story.

"It won't matter if that's what almost everyone else does. It'll still get twisted around." Christine exhaled heavily. "What should I do? I'd really rather not quit my job and go on the lam."

"Are you seeing anyone now?"

The question caught her off guard. "Oh, yes—in all of my free time, I have an exciting social life where I juggle countless men effortlessly." The corner of his mouth quirked up again but she was absolutely not looking at that smile. "This is it. I go to church. That's my social life. Even if I had time to date, finding a man who doesn't consider my daughter a roadblock to romance is challenging." His piercing stare made her nervous. "Why? You're not going to suggest that I get a boyfriend, are you? Or…"

He wasn't about to suggest that *he* become her boyfriend, was he? Because a man she didn't trust offering to protect her from a media frenzy by pretending to be a romantic interest—that seemed like a setup.

"Absolutely not," he said quickly. "That would only add fuel to the fire. No, I don't want you to find a boyfriend or a fiancé. Instead, I want you to keep doing what you always do."

"You want me to be boring?"

Something deepened in his eyes and, fool that she was, she wanted to think it was approval. "I want you to be the most boring person in the world, Christine." More flutters set off along her stomach at the way he said her name, but she ignored them. "The news cycle moves fast—even faster than it did two years ago. Doing anything interesting—including suddenly developing a love life—would only prolong your time in the spotlight."

They were back to awkward again. Because there was no way to convince her it wasn't awkward to have a man casually dismissing the possibility of her social life. Even though she knew he was right. "Got it. No fun."

He looked almost sympathetic at that. "You're not going to like this next part."

"I haven't liked any part so far."

He dropped his gaze and looked guilty again. It was unsettling. "I've already taken a number of steps to insulate you from the worst of the damage."

He was right. She didn't like the sound of that. "What kind of steps?"

Marie demanded her attention. When Christine looked back at Daniel, he was staring at her again. He needed to stop doing that. She was already struggling to not lust after him and having him look like he actually cared what happened to her wasn't helping. "I've arranged with a freelance journalist to flood the internet with articles that will drive down less positive articles about you in the search results. I've set up a phone number and email address so your phone at work isn't ringing off the hook and I've assigned a twenty-four-hour security detail to you."

She gaped at him, stunned. "You did *what*?"

For a moment, he looked uncomfortable. "I also know the names of the people currently tailing you and I'm working to make sure they leave you alone. I've already had one of them arrested on an outstanding warrant, but someone else will replace him, I'm sure."

She began to shake again with impotent anger. Which part of this was worse—the fact that he'd "taken the liberty" to set up phone numbers in her name or that the people who had been following her and Marie were the kind of people who had outstanding warrants?

None of it was good. "You did all of that without my permission?"

"Yes."

"After I told you to leave me alone?"

He didn't look away. "Yes."

She stood abruptly, gathering Marie to her chest. "Explain to me again why I'm supposed to trust you?"

He stood as well, his hands in his pockets. He looked contrite, but it was probably an act. "You need me, Christine."

"That's no explanation at all." Marie started to fuss. Christine grabbed her puffy coat and shoved the little girl's arms into it. "Why did you even ask me to meet with you, if you weren't going to listen to me anyway? God, I am *so* tired of other people deciding for me."

She spun on her heels to walk away, but Daniel's hand closed around her arm, bringing her to a halt. She could feel the warmth of his body heat through her sweater but it didn't matter. None of it mattered. "Let me go."

"Christine."

Then she made the mistake of looking at him. His eyes—they were huge and pleading and she didn't see dishonesty there. Why was the one man who gave a damn about her the one who'd ruined her life? It wasn't fair.

"And stop saying my name like that, darn it."

He was genuinely confused. "Like what?"

"Like I mean something to you. Because I don't. *We* don't. Stay away from me, Mr. Lee. Stop trying to rescue me from your own guilt."

She jerked away from him and this time, he didn't stop her. Marie looked back over her shoulder as Christine all but ran for the stairs and called out, *"anal grr!"* as she waved goodbye.

Christine was so mad that she struggled to keep the

tears from spilling over as she rushed out to her car. Because she couldn't cry. Someone might be watching. Doing something as unforgivably human as having a bad day would doom Christine to yet more hell on earth.

So, despite her anger and frustration and the sheer hopelessness, she kept a big smile pasted on her face, just in case someone was watching. Even if that someone was Daniel Lee. She wouldn't give him the satisfaction of knowing he'd upset her.

He was perfect and he was one hundred percent wrong and somehow, he was both of those things at the exact same time. He'd gotten her into this mess and she wanted nothing more than for him to make it go away, too.

But only fools clung to hopes and prayers and Christine was done being made the fool by any man. No more.

God, she hoped she never saw that man again.

Five

Over the course of the next week, Daniel tried to stop thinking about Christine.

He couldn't, actually. Because even though his actions had infuriated her, he still couldn't bring himself to abandon her to the winds of fate. She didn't have to like it and she didn't have to like him. But he was not going to let her be dragged through the muck and he especially was not going let Marie be dragged. The little girl was too innocent—and too helpless.

So he tried to think about her as a client—a non-paying one, but still, one who required a high level of personalized service without any active involvement in…anything.

It didn't work. Because although he was usually perfectly able to separate his personal life from his business endeavors, he was struggling this time.

He couldn't stop thinking about the way Christine had looked at him during their meeting—cautious and wary, then warm and happy when her little girl had mangled an animated tiger's name. Repeatedly. That smile—God. And she had no idea what she did to him, either.

It'd been a long time since he'd felt this kind of attraction to a woman. And even then, it wasn't the same. This wasn't merely an awareness of Christine on a sexual level. He was concerned about her. He wanted to make up for what he'd done, yes—but he didn't just want to shield her from the fallout. He wanted...

Hell, he didn't know what he wanted. Something more from her.

And he couldn't stop thinking about Marie, either. He hadn't expected how deeply it would affect him to hold the little girl on his lap and smell her baby smell and listen to her babble at him.

So, yeah—he was going to keep right on protecting the Murray women, whether Christine liked it or not. If anything happened to Marie because of something he'd started two years ago, he wasn't sure he could live with himself.

The hell of it was, he'd always been able to live with himself. So what was it about Christine and her daughter that was different? Had he gone soft?

If he was being honest, the situation struck a chord with him. Because the truth was, he knew what it was to grow up with a shadow permanently following him. Every time his mother had put him on the airplane to fly to Korea for the summer, he'd had to lock a part of himself away in a small box where his grandfather wouldn't be able to get to him.

He'd had to. His grandfather would never let Daniel forget that he was a bastard. As if Daniel had any choice in the matter. He hadn't, but that hadn't saved him from the old man's ire. No matter what he had done, no matter how hard he had worked, he had always been a stain on the Lee family honor.

He didn't want that for Marie. And if White or someone else made that child into a campaign issue, the stain of her birth—the stain Daniel had made—would follow her for the rest of her life. Those internet stories would never die. Marie would never have the chance to be her own person instead of the person everyone had already decided she was.

Just like he had made an executive decision two years ago about who Christine Murray was—a wild child, an embarrassment to her father's name. She'd been a liability. He'd turned up the witnesses with stories of parties and drinking. He'd dug up the truth about her pregnancy and he had constructed a fiction around those things—an out-of-control girl who was a risk to everyone around her.

She'd spent the last year and a half trying to live down that reputation. All because of him.

So he kept Porter Cole on the case and he kept his sister-in-law Natalie busy manipulating web rankings. He crafted several statements that he could put out on Christine's behalf. And he monitored the media requests. Occasionally, he had to contact a customer over a legitimate banking request who'd looked up Christine's number online, but that was an inconvenience he was willing to bear.

If Christine knew Daniel had hacked into her bank's website and changed two numbers on the direct line listed for her, she would kill him. At the very least, she might have him arrested. But given that he had racked up an impressive four hundred and thirty seven messages in a week, he was willing to risk that. Besides, her bosses would fail to appreciate it if their employee's phone rang so much that she couldn't do her job.

Maybe he was working overtime to justify his intrusion

into her life. But every time he felt bad about that, he'd remember the way Marie had waved goodbye to him and then another news article with a click-bait headline would pop up and Daniel would renew his resolve.

But most of all, he stayed alert. The campaign hadn't even really begun yet. These first few articles had merely been warning shots across the bow. The next attack would be coming soon and he needed to be ready.

"Daniel?"

Daniel started, then realized his brother Zeb stood in the doorway looking concerned. "Yes?"

"I said, is everything all right?"

Daniel let that question hang in the air for a moment. He and Zeb had been working together for almost a year, first to get control of the brewery and then to actually run it. But as for having a close brotherly relationship, that was still a work in progress. "Fine. Why do you ask?"

He could tell Zeb was trying not to laugh. "Oh, no reason. I've only been standing here for three minutes, trying to get your attention. Casey wants to get your opinion on the new pale ale brews. Do you have time?"

Zeb had married the brewmaster of the Beaumont Brewery. Together, she and Zeb had remade the Beaumont Brewery into a family business all over again. Daniel would like to take credit for that, but he wouldn't. He never did.

"Of course." He had been—well, not exactly neglecting his duties as the executive vice-president of the Beaumont Brewery—but he had certainly been distracted recently. If Zeb was noticing, it had become a problem.

Daniel stood, putting on his suit jacket. But before he could get the button buttoned, an alert chimed on his computer. "One second."

"She Tricked Me." The Father Of Clarence Murray's Granddaughter Speaks Out.

A sharp stabbing pain began to beat behind his eyeballs. Wasn't it a little early for this? It'd been less than two weeks since Murray had announced his candidacy.

"What's the matter?"

Daniel looked up at his brother. "Nothing."

"Are you sure?" Zeb leaned forward. "Because you look like someone just killed your dog and if it's something that affects you, it's something that affects me."

It was a noble sentiment. In fact, Daniel was pretty sure he had said something along those lines to Zeb when they had first joined forces to get control of the brewery. He had positioned himself as the all-knowing, all-seeing Beaumont bastard. He couldn't be surprised and he always had a plan.

He needed a better plan because no amount of misdirected phone numbers or web ranking manipulations were going to bury this particular lede.

"It's nothing," he repeated. He wasn't surprised that someone had gone after Marie's father—but he was disappointed that he hadn't gotten to the man first. "It's something going back to my previous career. It doesn't affect you or the brewery at all."

Zeb looked like he was debating whether or not to accept that statement at face value. "You'd tell me if you're in trouble?"

"I'm not." Zeb gave him a long look and, against his better judgment, Daniel buckled. "I'm just helping a friend." Although Christine would probably string him up by his toenails if she heard him describe her as a friend. The alerts chimed again—damn it. This was about to snowball. "Look, I need to deal with this. My apologies to Casey about the beer."

He grabbed his coat and started texting before he even got to the door. Bradley needed to bring the car around *now*.

As he brushed past Zeb, the man put a hand on Daniel's arm and stopped him. "She must mean a great deal to you, this friend."

That was a fishing expedition if Daniel had ever heard one. Zeb was a brilliant businessman, but he didn't seriously think that a leading question like that would get him anywhere, did he? "I'll keep you apprised of my whereabouts."

Zeb's eyebrows jumped. "Are you going to be gone for a while?"

"I don't know." Daniel thought he'd had a little more time than this. But watching and waiting was over. He needed to secure Christine and Marie. He didn't want to leave it to Porter or his associates.

He and Christine might not be friends, but he was beginning to think she might mean something to him, anyway.

Christine had thrown herself into work for the last week. She had loan applications to process, credit checks to run, a teething toddler who drooled more than the Mississippi River—more than enough to keep her busy. There was no time in her life to think about Daniel Lee, much less her father's political campaign. She didn't even go on the internet on her work computer unless she was specifically looking for something online. Ignorance was bliss and she simply did not want to know what her father or anyone connected with Missouri politics was doing at any given moment. To heck with whatever they said about her. She wouldn't give them any power over her and that was final.

It was a nice idea.

She still couldn't believe Daniel Lee was having her watched. Or that he was manipulating the internet, somehow. But she was forced to admit that, whatever he was doing, it appeared to be working. She hadn't seen anyone unusual loitering around her apartment or the day care. Her work phone had stopped ringing off the hook. In fact, she had gotten almost no phone calls for the last week, which was odd. Not that she was complaining. In fact, she was kind of relieved.

Maybe she wouldn't hate him. She found herself going over the way he'd let Marie read him a story, the way he'd laughed at her mispronunciations.

The way the heat of his hand had warmed Christine through her clothes and the way his eyes had watched her.

The way he'd looked at her like she mattered.

He was so far out of her league—that much was obvious. And lusting after the man—no matter how deeply she buried that lust—would only complicate every single problem in her life.

Besides, she didn't trust him. Or like him. Only a fool would crush on the man.

"Christine?"

Shaking herself out of her reverie, she looked up to see Sue standing before her, looking seriously worried. At the exact same moment, she realized that there was a dull roar coming from downstairs. "What's wrong?"

"There are reporters in the lobby," Sue said in confusion. "They're demanding to see you?"

"What?"

Just then, her phone buzzed. She looked at it in confusion. Where are you? It was from Daniel.

That realization, coupled with the fact that there were reporters in the building, made the bottom of her stomach fall out. "What's happening?" she asked Sue in a shaky whisper.

"I don't know," Sue replied, twisting her fingers together. "Mr. Whalen is trying to get them out of the building. But there's a *lot* of them. Some of them have really big cameras. Are you going to talk to them?"

Christine knew how this worked because this was what had happened last time. She'd been trying to come to grips with Doyle's sudden reluctance to set a date for their wedding even though she was four months pregnant when she had left work to find a reporter lying in wait for her, shouting rude questions about her pregnancy and her father's campaign. She hadn't known then that she had just become a centerpiece of the opponent's campaign. All she had known was that it felt like she was being attacked—because she was. By Daniel Lee.

This was no different. Those people expected her to come down there and maybe offer some weak statement of innocence or something. And then they would descend upon her like a pack of dogs and she was nothing but fresh meat for the next round of web hits.

"Absolutely not." She wished she had told Sue or even her bosses that this was a possibility. But denial wasn't just a river in Egypt.

Her phone buzzed again. Christine. Please let me help you.

She wanted to hate Daniel so much right now. But she needed help more. There are reporters downstairs. I don't want to talk to them.

"What are you going to do?" Sue asked, staring nervously over her shoulder as the volume downstairs increased.

Is there another way out of the building?

Yes. There was a staff exit by the drive-up windows.

A picture popped up in the text window of a gruff-looking man with a flattop and square jaw. It was followed by the text, This is Porter. He's a private investigator who works for me. Do you feel comfortable getting into a car with him?

The ludicrousness of the situation began to catch up with her. Maybe she should just go back and hide in the ladies' room. It didn't make any less sense than getting into a strange car with a strange investigator who was being paid by a strange man to protect her from her father's insanity.

Maybe this was how Alice felt when she sat down for tea with the Mad Hatter and the March Hare. Because Christine felt like there should be rules, a code of conduct for governing behavior—and nobody but her was trying to make those rules apply.

No, she texted back.

I'm fifteen minutes away. Will you feel safe getting into a car with me?

He was already on his way? He was coming here—for her? Where are we going if I get into a car with you? She was being snippy, but she couldn't help it. Once again, control over her life had been ripped away from her and this time she wasn't even sure why.

Well, to heck with that. She opened a web browser and searched. Immediately, she saw what the problem was.

"She Tricked Me." The Father of Clarence Murray's Granddaughter Speaks Out.

Dear God, Doyle had talked. Worse, she scrolled through the article and saw that he had included one of the pictures Christine had sent him from Marie's first birthday party. The very same picture that sat on her desk, crisp and clear for all the world to see.

White-hot rage blurred out everything but Marie's happy little face. She was going to *kill* Doyle. That was all there was to it. The man did not deserve to live after throwing his own daughter to the wolves.

Waves of fury and fear crashed into each other inside of her head, leaving her with a dull roaring in her ears. That also could be the reporters clamoring downstairs.

"Christine? Sue asked, looking like she was on the verge of crying.

"I'm going to leave," she told her best friend. "A friend of mine is going to pick me up and we're going to go. Somewhere." She didn't know where but, given the racket coming from downstairs, she almost didn't care.

Christine? Daniel texted her.

I'm not sure safe is the right word, but I can't stay here and face these reporters.

Thirteen minutes away. I'll have Porter create a disturbance.

Thirteen minutes. She could make it thirteen minutes, right? Come to the drive-up window.

Then she looked up at Sue. Sue, who was only a few inches taller than Christine and heavyset. Sue, who had overhighlighted her hair, making it blondish. Sure, Sue had a square jaw and brown eyes and freckles and was bottom-heavy instead of top-heavy like Christine was. The women didn't really look that much alike. But to someone who didn't know either of them…

Sue was close enough.

"Christine?"

"Sue, I need a favor," she said, digging out her sunglasses and handing over her knit cap. "I need your winter coat and you're going to take mine."

"What? Why?"

I have a distraction, she texted to Daniel. Then, to Sue, she added, "You're going to pretend to be me."

Six

Daniel wasn't sure if Christine's bait and switch was going to work. She claimed her coworker bore a passing resemblance to her. In a flurry of texts, Daniel had arranged for Porter to muscle his way into the bank, escort the other woman to his car, and drive off. After five or ten minutes, Porter would switch vehicles, come back to the drive-through, and hopefully, the coworker would slip back into the building with no one else the wiser.

But then what? For the first time in a very long time, Daniel didn't have a plan A, plan B or even a plan C.

He was getting soft. That was the only possible explanation for why he hadn't planned for this contingency.

There were two different ways to get to the drive-through—the parking lot and the alley. As Bradley swung around to the second entrance, Daniel could see the crowd churning in the parking lot, like sharks at a feeding frenzy. He just caught a glimpse of Porter muscling people aside, a smallish woman tucked under his arm, when the car turned into the alley, bringing it to the drive-through. He rolled down his window as the teller behind the glass said, "May I help you?"

"I'm picking up a delivery." As the words crackled across the microphone, he saw Christine peek around the corner, an unfamiliar hat scrunched low over her head.

The teller shut off the microphone and turned. She and Christine said a few words, then Christine pulled the hat down even lower, completely obscuring her blond hair.

A minute later, a small side door opened and she slipped out. Daniel did a quick look around, but he didn't see any reporters lying in wait. Christine came around the side of the vehicle, opened the door and climbed in. The moment she shut the door behind her, Bradley began to drive.

"Are you all right?" Daniel asked after a moment of silence.

"Oh, sure. It's just the end of the world. I'll be fine." Christine said the whole thing in a monotone voice.

Was she quoting song lyrics? "You're in shock."

That caught her attention. She rolled her head to look at him and then kept right on rolling her eyes. "Do you think? I'm at least glad to see you're not texting and driving." She looked around at the car. "I was sort of expecting you to be in a little sports car."

For some reason, this response made him grin. She hadn't given up. She still had a lot of fight in her and, oddly, he was glad to see her. "We could change, if you'd like. Would you rather avoid the press in a Corvette or a Maserati?"

"I was joking."

Daniel felt his grin grow. "I wasn't. But to do that, we would have to go back to my place and I'm not sure you'd be comfortable doing that." Oddly, though, he wanted her to be comfortable with it. If he had her back at his condo, there would be additional levels of security between her and the rest of the world.

"I'm not comfortable doing any of this. But I can't just sit there and wait for them to find me again."

"I agree."

She exhaled heavily, staring out the window. "I suppose this is the moment you tell me that it's not safe for me to go home?"

Guilt hit him again, a feeling he didn't want and didn't have time to deal with. "If you'd really like to go home, I am more than happy to take you there. However, I don't feel that's the safest option for you."

"Because they already know where I live?"

She was not going to like this. Daniel braced for the worst. "Because someone has already tried to break into your place."

She jolted as if he had jabbed her with a pin. "What? When?"

"Before we met at the church. My associate scared the guy off. They did not gain access to your apartment or your personal things, but I realize that must be little comfort to you now."

She squeezed her eyes shut tight as the blood drained from her face and Daniel wished he could stop being the bearer of bad news. He wished he had never heard the name Christine Murray. Or Clarence Murray, for that matter.

In that moment, he wished, for the first time in a very long time, that he had been someone else. Someone better. Someone who could have done and said the right things at the right time.

He wished that he were the kind of person who would've

protected someone like Christine the first time, instead of using her.

Sadly, he had very little idea of what a man like that would look like.

"Is this the part where I get to run away and hide?" she asked in a shaky voice. To his horror, a tear escaped her closed eyes and trickled down her cheek.

It hit him harder than any name she could've called him, any insult she could've shouted. And he would give anything to make it better.

He reached over and cupped her cheek, his thumb brushing that tear away. "Is that what you want?"

When she opened her eyes, the world stopped spinning. She looked at him with such longing and hopelessness all mixed together and he knew he needed to drop his hand away. But he couldn't. He couldn't leave her alone. "You know that you're the only man who asks me that? But I don't know what the point of answering it is. Because I still don't know if you listen to me and I still don't know why I should trust you."

"I want to make this better for you," he told her honestly, his thumb still moving over her cheek. It felt so unusual to be honest.

"Just because you feel guilty about what you did to me?"

Somehow, he was getting closer to her and he desperately wanted to believe she was getting closer to him, too. "No."

That's where it started—but that wasn't the position from which he was operating now.

"I want the world to go back to normal. I want to raise my daughter in peace and quiet. I want to do my job without fear that the next time the phone rings, it'll start all over again. That's what I want."

"It will," he promised her. "It just won't happen today. Or tomorrow."

Another tear slipped free and rolled down her cheek. "I should hate you," she said in a voice so soft he had to lean even closer to hear it. Only a few inches separated them now. "You ruined everything. Why don't I hate you?"

In some distant part of his mind, he was calculating the extensive list of reasons why she should hate him. But that list wasn't the reason he wiped this second tear away with his thumb, nor was it the reason he lifted her chin, pulling her closer. Because she didn't hate him. "Because I'm trying to take care of you."

This close, her eyes were an impossible shade of blue, like sapphires catching the light. And the fact that he was even thinking such trite thoughts about any woman— much less *this* woman—was so far out of character for him that he almost didn't recognize himself.

"Why?" Her breath was warm against his cheek. He was close enough to feel that breath, close enough to taste her.

He was going to. He forgot about campaigns and illegitimate children and breweries and terrible fathers. His hand slid down her cheek to her neck and he could feel her pulse throbbing just underneath her delicate skin— skin he wanted to press his lips against. For the few moments they had near privacy in the back of his car, he didn't want to think about the past or the future. Just her. Just him and her.

He brushed his lips over hers, a request more than a kiss. At first, he thought she was going to kiss him back— she sighed against his lips and leaned into him. When she did so, all he could think was *mine*.

Mine.

Then she pulled away, her cheeks blushing a brilliant

crimson. She snapped her gaze out the window and then startled again. "Wait—why are we here?"

Daniel forcibly shook back to himself. Had he lost his mind? Had he almost kissed Christine Murray in the backseat of his car as they were making a getaway of sorts?

She completely turned him around. Did she have any idea how hard it was to do that? He never lost control—or failed to see the big picture.

Except when it came to her, apparently.

"Ah. You didn't think I was going to help you disappear without getting your daughter, did you?"

Christine looked stunned as the driver pulled around the back of the day care. "What did you do?" she asked in that voice that he didn't like—distant and scared.

He didn't want her to feel like she had lost control of her life, even if she had. "I told them you would be picking Marie up early and if they could somehow find a car seat for her, that would be great."

Christine turned back to look at him. "They're going to think you're kidnapping us."

"I'm not. You know that, right? If you wanted, I could leave you here. I'll have Bradley and Porter bring you your car. I will leave you alone if you want me to, Christine." As the words hung in the air, he found himself fervently hoping that she wouldn't want him to.

An older woman with a helmet of curls peeked out the back door. That was probably Mrs. McDonald, the day care operator he'd spoken to on the phone. Christine shot a concerned look at Daniel, but then got out. Daniel let the women speak in private.

As he waited, he got a text from Porter that the investigator had safely returned Christine's coworker to the bank through the staff door. Most of the reporters had dispersed—but Porter warned they could be heading for the day care next.

They didn't have much time. Christine needed to decide what she wanted to happen next. Would she be able to trust him? And if she did, where would he take her? Denver wasn't safe. If someone connected him with her, it would only make the situation worse.

No, they had to go somewhere else. Somewhere where he was not the executive vice-president of the Beaumont Brewery and she was not Clarence Murray's daughter.

If it were just the two of them, he would fly her to Seoul. He maintained a condo in the city and usually spent at least a few weeks a year there, monitoring his business interests and honoring his grandparents' graves.

Christine went inside with Mrs. McDonald. No, he absolutely did not want to bustle a toddler onto a plane for an eighteen-hour flight. Which left only one option.

He called up the number of his pilot. "Lennon, get the jet ready. I'm leaving for Chicago and I'll have two guests, a woman and a baby. Please plan accordingly."

"Are you *sure* everything is okay?" Mrs. McDonald asked for the fifteenth time. "Because if it's not…"

Christine sighed. At this point, all she could do was hide but where would she go? She had limited funds for things like hotels and airline tickets.

"Everything is fine. Mr. Lee is a family friend. My father is in the news again and there were a bunch of reporters at work and I'm afraid that they're going to be on their way here next and I need to keep Marie safe. That's all this is."

When she said it like that, it all sounded perfectly reasonable.

Unlike that near kiss in the backseat of Daniel's very

expensive car. There hadn't been a single reasonable thing about that—not the way he'd touched her and not the way her body had responded to him and not the way that, even now, she wished she'd let him kiss her.

But Daniel had a driver, for God's sake, sitting right there in the front seat. She couldn't kiss Daniel with witnesses.

She was in Mrs. McDonald's office, a closet-sized room with a huge glass window so she could see who came and went from the Gingerbread Day Care. It was nap time and, for once, the building was quiet. "I just find it odd that a strange man calls up and asks me to find a child seat and get Marie ready and he's not on your preferred list. And then you show up with him in a car like that? You have to admit, Ms. Murray, that the whole thing is odd."

"Daniel is a friend," Christine repeated. "I promise there's nothing hinky about this."

God, how she wished that was true.

Mrs. McDonald fretted. "Well, if you say so." She led the way out of the tiny office to where all of the children were sprawled out on miniature cots.

Christine moved as if she were in a daze. Daniel had almost kissed her. In the movies, a kiss was a moment of clarity, a declaration. It made everything make sense.

This wasn't the movies and Christine had never been more confused in her entire life. Everything had spiraled out of control—including her good sense. Because Daniel Lee's lips should be nowhere near hers.

But there was one thing that hadn't changed—that was her daughter. Christine bent over Marie's sleeping form. "Honey, we're going for a ride, okay?" Marie didn't stir.

Mrs. McDonald appeared with Marie's backpack and a car seat that had seen better days. Christine lifted her daughter and the two women moved silently to the back door. Marie stirred in Christine's arms, so warm and heavy with sleep.

The driver, whose name Christine did not know, was waiting for them. He took the car seat from Mrs. McDonald and started to install it where Christine had been sitting.

At the same time, Daniel came over to speak to Mrs. McDonald. As Christine watched, he thanked her warmly and handed her a check for the car seat. He even made sure she had his cell phone number, inviting her to call at any time. He talked about this Porter Cole guy again, the private investigator who had apparently been watching Christine for some time. He promised Mrs. McDonald that, if anyone from the media showed up and started making a nuisance of themselves, Porter would help her handle it.

That was when Mrs. McDonald surprised Christine. "*The* Porter Cole? The hotshot detective that does all that work for the Beaumont family?" Honest to God, Mrs. McDonald's eyes lit up.

Christine had never heard of Porter—but then again, she wasn't exactly plugged into the heartbeat of the Denver social scene.

As Daniel and Mrs. McDonald discussed the private investigator, the driver got the car seat installed and Christine got Marie belted in. Daniel walked Christine around to the other side of the car and held the door for her, and then circled back around to sit in the passenger seat in front.

And just like that, they were off. Destination unknown.

She felt she should be panicking more but she was drained. "We're going by my apartment?"

"No. Not unless there's something that you absolutely cannot live without. Medicines, for example."

She got the feeling he was asking about birth control. She'd had an IUD installed after Marie's birth for obvious reasons. "No, no medicines." She rifled through Marie's backpack. Oh, thank goodness—there was Pooh Bear, her stuffed animal. "If we don't go back to the apartment, where are we going, Daniel?"

He turned around in the seat, his gaze meeting hers. "You want to disappear until this blows over, right?"

"Yes." But even as she said it, another wave of exhaustion hit her. Would this ever really blow over?

"Chicago, then. We're going to Chicago."

Her mouth fell open and she couldn't do anything but stare at him for a long moment. Then the moment got longer she tried to make sense of what he'd just said. "Chicago? As in, Illinois?"

An almost smile ghosted over his lips. "There's only one. I maintain a residence there. The other alternative was Seoul, South Korea—but I didn't think your daughter would do well on a flight that long."

She blinked. "You maintain a residence in South Korea?"

"Of course," he said, as if it was no big deal to own homes in multiple countries. "Now, if you're comfortable..." She began to laugh, but he ignored the outburst. "Could you give me your size and preferences for clothing and toiletries?"

God, just when she thought it couldn't get any worse—now this gorgeous, apparently filthy-rich man who had almost kissed her wanted to know what size she wore. "Why?"

"You can sleep in those clothes if you want, but I think you and your daughter will be more comfortable if you have a change of clothes. And Marie needs diapers?" It came out as a question.

Despite the insanity of it all, she smiled at him. "That would probably be a good idea. Can I make a list?" That way, at least, she wouldn't have to say *size twelve* out loud.

He nodded and produced a small notepad. She wrote down a basic list of things they would need and handed it over to him.

This wasn't a stretch limo so there was no partition dividing the front and the back. But after she handed over the list, it was almost as if a wall was raised between them. Marie had fallen back asleep once the car started to move and Daniel turned his attention to his phone. He was texting and then he made some calls. He spoke in a language she assumed was Korean.

He owned a home in Korea. In her internet searches, she hadn't turned up anything that even hinted at that.

It just reminded her once again that he knew practically everything about her—including her jeans size—and she knew practically nothing about him.

She looked out the window and realized that instead of heading north toward the Denver International Airport, they were heading south. "I thought you said we were flying to Chicago?"

"We are. I keep my private jet at Centennial Airport. It's easier."

She hadn't even realized there were other airports in Denver. Once again, she felt woefully out of her league. "You have a private jet?"

Daniel looked back at her over his shoulder and shot her a quick but intense smile. "Is this going to be a problem? If you changed your mind, we can make other plans."

"I don't think we can go to Seoul. Marie doesn't have a passport and mine might be expired and even if it wasn't, I'd have to look for it."

Besides, there were advantages to going to Chicago. There, no one probably cared about Beaumonts or Clarence Murray and his delusional quest for public office. No one could tail them in a private jet. And Chicago was a very big city. Maybe they would disappear into the teeming mass of humanity.

So she made her decision. "Chicago is fine."

He gave that little nod with his head that was almost more of a bow and then turned his attention back to his phone.

Christine reached over and covered Marie's hand with hers. This was a level of insane she had never anticipated—but if it managed to keep her daughter safe from the onslaught of reporters there'd been at the bank, it was worth it.

An hour later, they pulled onto a runway, right alongside of Daniel's private jet. It was sleek and powerful-looking, and in that way, it reminded her of Daniel. There wasn't anything wasted about it.

Marie woke up as they were unbuckling her and was now full of postnap energy and grumpiness. Luckily, a woman was waiting for them with a few bags of supplies, including a box of diapers. Daniel said a few words to her.

Christine watched as the woman got into a car and sped off. "Who was that?"

"Someone who works for me. Don't worry about it."

Christine snorted. "You realize that I'm about to get on a private jet with a man I barely know and a toddler who's never flown before because it's better than the alternative of waiting for the reporters to break into my house. What part of *that* am I not supposed to worry about?"

Daniel paused, his hand on the railing that led up the steps into his jet. "Christine, I know this is a difficult time, but I would never hurt you or your daughter."

She so desperately wanted to believe his words. "Again, you mean?"

The look of pain flashed over his face. "Again. Shall we?"

She was surprised to see a car seat already installed in

one of the leather chairs—chairs that were nicer than any furniture she owned. They swiveled and had extendable footrests and she was willing to bet the leather was Italian, just like his shoes. "You really do own your own jet."

"I do. Here." He held out his hands for Marie. "I'd recommend using the facilities before we take off."

"Good idea." But she didn't move immediately because she was busy looking at Daniel.

"Anal grr," Marie said in a sleepy voice as she lurched toward him.

The smile on Daniel's face hit Christine like a hammer because he looked so happy to see Marie, happier to be holding her. God help Christine, but Daniel looked like he really cared about her daughter. That feeling only got stronger when he said, "Hi, sweetie," in a tender voice as he tickled Marie's tummy. Marie giggled and Christine's heart clenched.

In another life, this would be everything she'd never allowed herself to dream of. A hot, rich man who cared about her and her daughter? Her fantasies definitely weren't this good.

But in this life, she hurried to the back of the plane to one of the nicest bathrooms she had ever been in. There was even a shower.

She took a moment after she was done to wash her face. There was still a chance this was a dream. Possibly a nightmare. She was going to wake up in her own bed in her own apartment with her own boring life stretching out before her. Marie would keep teething, they would keep working on potty training and hot, insanely rich guys wouldn't make what sounded like sincere promises to her. Because this wasn't her life any more than her father's strict rules and regulations for governing female behavior had been her life.

It was only when Christine realized that she was, once again, hiding out in the ladies' room that she forced herself back to the front of the plane. The door had been sealed, but the plane wasn't moving yet. Marie was cruising from chair to table to chair. And Daniel? Daniel was sitting on the floor, smiling wildly as Marie got grubby fingerprints all over his pristine plane.

If this was a dream, perhaps she didn't want to wake up. Perhaps she wanted to stay in this not-reality where an eligible, insanely rich man saved the day.

"Are you married?" she asked before she could stop the words from coming out of her mouth.

Daniel's eyebrows jumped up, but he didn't look like she had trapped him in a corner. "No. Despite my grandfather's best attempts to find me a proper wife to carry the family name, I remain unattached and uninvolved." Before she could make sense of *that* statement, Daniel rose to his feet. "If you'll excuse me, you might want to get Marie into her seat. We'll be taking off shortly."

"Oh. Sorry." Dying of self-inflicted embarrassment, she scooped Marie out of Daniel's way. Once the door had closed behind him, she looked around. The sofa would have to do as a changing table.

There was a blanket in the bags—Christine would've preferred to wash it first, but beggars couldn't be choosers. She laid it out on the sofa and quickly changed Marie's diaper.

"Baby," she tried to explain, "we're going to take a trip with Mr. Daniel. It's going to be a lot of fun." She hoped.

"Anal grr!"

Christine grinned. *"Daniel*, baby. Can you say Daniel?"

"ANAL!"

Christine couldn't help it. She began to laugh. There was no other response possible.

Really, getting into the car and then the plane with him—that was the sort of impulsive, half-baked thing she would've done back when she was a teenager. It had only been since Marie had arrived and Christine had been raked over the coals publicly that she had stopped acting out. If she weren't so worried, she would be enjoying the hell out of this.

Maybe that's what she needed to do—worry less, enjoy more. While it was still a possibility that Daniel could turn out to be an ax murderer, she doubted it. In fact, aside from the fact that he had openly admitted to destroying her life two years ago, he didn't seem particularly evil at all.

If that was as good as it got—not particularly evil—then that's what she was going with. Because the alternatives were not pretty. Brian White, who worked for her father? He was evil. And her father? Evil was a strong word but...

She got Marie strapped into her new car seat and found a bag of Goldfish crackers from the supplies that Daniel's associate had provided. There was a sippy cup as well. Christine noticed there was a wet bar tucked back in the corner near the bathroom, so she quickly rinsed out the cup. Next to the wet bar, there were several mini fridges tucked under a cabinet. In one there was a variety of alcohol—including stuff that looked really expensive. He flew with champagne? Was that even a good idea? But in the other one there were more normal beverages—soda, sparkling water and apple juice. Bingo.

She filled the sippy cup. She turned back to Marie just as the door to the bathroom opened and Daniel emerged. They almost collided, but he caught her in time. "Ah," he said, taking in the sippy cup. "I see you're finding your way around."

"It's not that big of a plane." His hand was still on her arm and she was blushing terribly.

His eyes crinkled with what she hoped was amusement. "Size isn't everything, or so I've heard."

He was teasing her, she realized. Teasing her and rubbing small circles on her inner arm with his thumb. The flush of embarrassment caught and flamed into something hotter. Something needier.

How long had it been? Too danged long.

"Thank you," she said softly.

Something in his eyes shifted. How could he look at her like that? Like she was somehow glamorous and desirable instead of a disaster with a daughter?

His head tilted toward hers, but he didn't kiss her. He didn't even come close to it—not this time. "Thank you for trusting me." Before she could respond to that, he took the sippy cup and went to sit down by Marie.

No, if this was a dream, she definitely didn't want to wake up.

Seven

"Oh, thank goodness," Christine said, exhaustion in her voice as she slumped back into the plush seating of Daniel's Chicago car.

This Mercedes was longer than his Denver car, the better to accommodate the divider between the driver and the passengers.

"I have to ask—is it always that much fun?" He didn't know a lot about babies but it'd been obvious that Marie had not enjoyed her first flight.

Christine shot him a weak smile. "Sometimes, it's even more entertaining. She's teething. She hasn't figured out yet how to tell me she doesn't feel good without crying. The doctor says she's normal." She notched an eyebrow at him, her eyes tired. "Didn't you grow up with any brothers and sisters?"

"No." That was all he would've said to anyone else, but Christine gave him a measured look and he remembered her saying that he knew everything about her and she knew nothing about him. "My mother never married and she was an only child. And, as you know, I didn't grow up with any of my half siblings on my father's side."

She gave him a tired smile. What was it about that look that made him want to pull her into his arms and let her rest? Maybe she could relax at the condo. There, at least, no reporters would be lying in wait. Plus, Chicago did have one advantage over Seoul, Korea—his mother, Minnie.

But even as he thought it, he worried. His mother had been almost as bad as his grandfather about wanting grandchildren. Daniel had refused to get married in Korea, no matter what his grandfather said. He wouldn't give the old man the satisfaction.

His mother, however, was a different matter entirely. She didn't want grandchildren to carry on the Lee family name and restore the Lee family honor.

She wanted grandchildren because she wanted *grandchildren*. And here he was, bringing an adorable baby girl and a single mother back to his condo. Would his mother restrain herself?

Christine slumped back in her seat. "I grew up in Missouri—we had our own local brewery with its own family drama. I don't know very much about the Beaumonts."

It was a relief. Being an acknowledged Beaumont brought a measure of personal scrutiny that he didn't enjoy. "There's not much to know."

She lifted her head up and squinted at him through one eye.

"My family legacy—my American family, that is— was something we didn't talk about growing up," he said.

He hadn't even known who his father was until he'd turned six. Apparently, being in kindergarten had made him mature enough in Lee Dae-Won's eyes to inform him that his real father was a heartless businessman from Colorado who, along with Daniel's mother, had stained the Lee family honor.

But he pushed that frustration away because Christine had rested her head back against the seat. He thought she might fall asleep—which was fine. Given current traffic conditions, they had about an hour from the airport to his condo on the lakefront. She needed the rest.

What he really wanted to do was slide into the seat next to her, wrap his arm around her shoulders and tuck her in close. He wanted to physically take the burden from her shoulders and let her know she was safe with him.

He also wanted to finish the kiss they'd started in Colorado. Which was not the same as making sure she felt safe. In fact, he was pretty sure those two desires didn't mesh at all.

So he did the only thing he could do—he stayed on his side of the car. He couldn't allow this attraction to distract him from the matter at hand—deflecting media attention and protecting the Murray women. He'd just taken out his phone to check his messages when she spoke again. "Was it rough, growing up without any contact with your father or his family?"

The question took him by surprise. No one had ever asked that question before. Not even Zeb.

He didn't answer fast enough, because she went on, "I'm sorry if I'm prying. Marie's father doesn't want anything to do with her, either. Or," she added with a bitter laugh, "he didn't, until he realized he could use her for his own aims."

He set his phone down. "It wasn't bad. It wasn't as good as CJ had it—you know CJ, my other half brother?"

"I used to watch *A Good Morning With Natalie Baker* when I first moved here. She married him, right?"

"Yes, that brother. His mother married and he had a

happy childhood. But I think that's rare for anyone, to have two parents who are completely committed to making sure you have a stable upbringing. The fact that I had one parent committed to that was a gift. I think you're going to be that person for Marie, too."

Her head popped up. "You think?"

He couldn't fight the grin if he'd wanted to—and he didn't want to. "I *know*. You're an amazing mom doing the best you can with what you've got—even if what you've got is a toxic relative with deep pockets."

With a groan, she let her head fall back again. "Don't remind me." There was another moment of silence before she added, "How much worse is this going to get?"

"Actually, now that we're on ground level, I think it's only going to get better from here."

She snorted, an indelicate noise that made him smile. "I wasn't talking about Marie screaming. I was talking about the scandal. About what's happening between us."

Daniel froze, but she still wasn't looking at him. There wasn't anything happening between them.

All right, in a misguided attempt to comfort her earlier, he had touched her. And almost kissed her. And yes, he had flown her across the country and was actively taking her to his condominium—where he had never brought a woman before. And, sure—his mother was going to be waiting there to meet them and would undoubtedly take one look at Marie and fall head over heels in love.

None of that meant anything was happening between *them*.

Really.

He exhaled heavily. Perhaps if he kept telling himself that lie, he might even start believing it.

Because the truth was, it did feel like something was happening, something strange and unexpected. He had started this endeavor from a position of weakness—he had allowed himself to feel guilt over his actions. Christine didn't seem to realize how unusual that was—maybe it was better that she didn't. Maybe he didn't want her to know how much of a coldhearted bastard he could be. She knew enough, anyway.

He didn't have an answer for her so he kept quiet, hoping she would doze off. And it seemed like that was what happened because she was silent for several minutes. Then, out of nowhere, her voice came again. "I still don't know why you're doing this."

She sounded sleepy and he had an overwhelming urge to be the soft place where she could land. He had never had that particular urge before. "Maybe you don't have to know why."

"That's a load of malarkey."

Even though she couldn't see it, he cracked a wide grin. "Malarkey? That's not a word you hear every day."

"I have this daughter, you see. She has a tendency to pick up on words and repeat them loudly when it's most inconvenient." She lifted her head and cracked one eye open. "Do I need to remind you about the Daniel Tiger incident?"

He chuckled. "Trust me, I won't ever forget the Daniel Tiger incident."

She was looking at him again with both eyes now. "Why, Daniel?"

"I didn't want to be another person who let you down." This was the problem with honesty. Once a person started being honest, it became almost addictive. There was a certain measure of freedom in the truth. He felt like he could breathe.

Something in the air changed between them, charging the space in the limo with electricity. "I don't want you to be another person who lets me down," she said softly.

For too much of his life, he had been concerned with his own interests. And his mother's, of course. He was even concerned with his grandfather's business interests—up to a point. He wasn't going to marry anyone for family honor—but Lee Enterprises had made Daniel an insanely wealthy man.

He cared for his siblings—in a fashion. It was in his best interest to keep his siblings protected and the family business solvent.

But what did he have to gain from Christine? What was in it for him to shield Marie?

Nothing. He knew it and Christine knew it, too. He had nothing to gain by doing any of this.

Funny how that hadn't stopped him yet.

"I won't be." It wasn't an empty promise but, given the worry that crept into the corner of Christine's eyes, he wasn't sure that she believed him.

Which was smart. She should absolutely not put her full faith and trust in him. She should keep her guard up.

But he wanted that trust. Suddenly, he needed it.

The car turned and Daniel became aware of his surroundings. They were on Lower Wacker Drive, turning toward Navy Pier.

Quickly, Daniel checked his messages. There were no emergencies from Zeb, so that was good. Natalie had forwarded him several new links to articles that were full of content scraped from Marie's father's original interview. Some days, it was like playing whack-a-mole on the internet.

"Where are we?" Christine asked.

"Home." Huang, his driver, pulled into the garage and parked at the entrance. The doorman had the door open before Christine could blink.

"Welcome home, Mr. Lee."

"It's good to be home, Rowell. These are my guests. They have complete access to my condo." Behind him, he heard Christine give a little squeak. The staff here was highly trained to keep their mouths shut. He turned and held out a hand.

After a moment's hesitation, she took it and let him help her to her feet. "Hello," she said nervously to the doorman.

"We have a few things in the trunk." With a small salute, Rowell went to the trunk. Daniel leaned in to unbuckle Marie. The little girl startled as he lifted her out and handed her to her mother. Christine tucked her daughter to her chest, rubbing her back. It was such a sweet image that Daniel wished he could take a picture of it.

What would it be like, if this were real? If he were returning with his wife and daughter after a business trip, everyone tired and happy to be home? They'd go upstairs and unpack, give Marie a bath and, once the little girl was asleep, he and Christine would...

Would *what*? Fall into bed, taking comfort in each other? No. He didn't take comfort from anyone, much less a woman who was still well within her rights to view his every single action as suspect. Even if he wanted to strip her out of her rumpled business suit and make love to her until she was sated, he couldn't get any closer.

He shook his head at his own foolishness. He was about to introduce Christine to his mother. It didn't get much closer than that.

In short order, he was leading them down the hall to his corner condo. Before he could get his keys out, the door swung open and there stood his mother, hope all over her face.

This was a mistake, but it was too late now.

"Dae-Hyun," she said, using his real name. *"Naega geogjeonghaessda." I was worried.*

That was just like her, to worry about him despite the fact that he'd been in Denver for a few months. Even though she had lived in Chicago for almost thirty-five years, she spoke Korean with him when they were alone.

Daniel stepped inside and kissed his mother on the cheek. *"Annyeong eomma,"* he said, telling her hi. Then he stepped to the side and switched to English. "Mom, I'd like to introduce you to Christine Murray and her daughter, Marie."

Her eyes lit up as she turned to Christine and Marie. "Welcome," she said, her English softly accented. Mom bowed in their direction. Daniel had been embarrassed by that bow when he was growing up. It had always marked his mother as a foreigner. But now, it was comforting. "I'm so glad Daniel brought you for a visit."

Which was a nice way of phrasing "mad dash to get away from the press." He snorted. "Christine, this is my mother, Minnie Lee."

"Hello," Christine said nervously, clutching Marie to her chest. Her gaze cut back to Daniel.

He set down the bags his assistant, Beth, had gotten them for the airplane ride. "Mom, have the other things been delivered yet?"

Minnie didn't hear him. She had eyes for one person and one person only. "Oh," she cooed, stepping in to place a hand on Marie's back. "Was the plane ride very hard?"

Christine glanced over his mother's head—which was saying something, because Christine was not that tall to begin with—and made eye contact with Daniel. He could see the second she made up her mind, the tension in her eyes fading as she smiled a warm smile at his mother. "It was a little bit of a rough flight. She's never been on an airplane before."

Mom clucked sympathetically. "You must be so tired. Both of you. I have some snacks in the kitchen. Some fresh fruit and milk? You could take a few moments to freshen up. I had a guest room set up for you."

Christine blinked in surprise at this, but Minnie turned back to Daniel. "The crib proved to be a problem, but they sent over a portable one." She turned back to Christine. "I hope that will be all right?"

"Um…yes?"

Mom's eyes crinkled with warmth. "Come with me. I'm so glad Daniel brought you here," she repeated.

As if Daniel hadn't already known this was a mistake, that sentence sealed the deal. His mother was already painting rosy pictures of happy babies and little grand-daughters.

With another look, Christine followed Minnie into the apartment. He heard her gasp when she rounded the corner and saw the view. When he caught up with her in the living room, she was standing openmouthed and staring out at the never-ending sky. "This is amazing."

"I like it."

Which was something of an understatement. He liked being above everyone on the top floor. He liked looking down on Navy Pier, at the scurrying little dots that were the rest of humanity. He liked being unreachable and un-touchable—and of course the privacy that went with both of those things.

Christine turned to his mother. "How long have you lived here?"

His mother's laugh tinkled lightly. "Oh, I don't live here. This is Dae-Hyun's home. I live in Wheeling."

When Christine looked confused by this statement, Daniel added, "That's close to where we landed. Mom volunteers at the Korean Cultural Center located there."

"Oh. Okay." He could tell that it still didn't make much sense to her.

At that moment, Marie seemed to come fully awake. She squirmed in Christine's arms. Christine tried to set her down and hold on to her hand, but the little girl was a lot faster than she looked. She fell to her hands and knees and crawled over to the windows, where she got back to her feet and began cruising and banging on the glass. "Pretty!" she crowed.

Christine gasped, but Daniel put a hand on her arm. "That glass is inches thick. She is not going to knock it out. I promise."

Mom hurried over and crouched down beside the little girl. "Pretty, isn't it?"

Marie turned a wide smile to the older woman and Daniel felt something tighten in his chest. It only got worse when his mother clapped her hands and giggled like a schoolgirl.

He leaned down and spoke softly in Christine's ear. "I think the two of them will be fine for a few minutes. Would you like to see your room?"

She nodded and, without taking his hand away from her arm, he led her through his apartment. He pointed out things like the kitchen and the dining room—which was really an extension of the living room. Then he led her down the hall to the extra bedrooms. "I keep a room here for Mom when she wants to stay in town but she won't be here tonight, so you can take her room," he explained. "I have two other guestrooms, but I use one as an office. So you'll have to let me know if you want Marie to stay in the room with you or if you would like her to be next door." He showed her the bathrooms and then opened the door to the guestroom.

"You really do live here," Christine said, a note of

amazement in her voice as she stepped away from him to look around.

"Yes, I do. Did you think I would bring you to some dungeon and keep you locked away?"

She shot him a look. "I hadn't ruled it out. And besides, you don't need a dungeon to keep someone trapped."

"You're free to leave whenever you want," he said, stepping closer. Too close. He was close enough to touch her now and that was exactly what he did. He took her bag from her shoulder and set it on the bed, next to the boxes he'd ordered from Saks Fifth Avenue.

For the second time today, he brushed his fingertips over her cheek. She didn't pull away—although she didn't exactly throw herself into his arms, either. Instead, she stood looking at him as if he were a space alien. "But I'd like you to stay for a little while."

That was the wrong thing to say. But he wasn't sure what the right thing would have been. She took in a shuddering breath and stepped back. "You shouldn't look at me like that."

"Like what?"

"Like...*that*." She waved her hand in the air, as if that magically explained anything. The color rose in her cheeks. "You know."

"No, I don't."

Now she waved both hands in the air, looking like a panicked bird. "You're being intentionally obtuse. You shouldn't look at me like you *like* me because we both know you don't."

Now it was his turn to blink at her in wonder. "Whatever gave you that idea?"

"Seriously?"

"Putting aside the events of several years ago—"

She snorted. "That's one way to put it."

Daniel pressed on, undeterred. "When have I given you the impression at any point in the last several weeks that I don't like you?"

He really was trying to understand. And failing.

"You can stop making fun of me now." She turned to walk out of the bedroom.

"Christine."

Eight

He put a hand on her shoulder to stop her. "I am *not* making fun of you."

"Aren't you? What other possible explanation could there be?"

He stepped close enough to brush her hair away from her cheek. "Has it ever occurred to you that I'm attracted to you?"

He didn't know how he'd expected her to react to that statement—but barking out a bitter laugh wasn't it. "Oh, that's rich. How could a man like you be attracted to a woman like me?"

Daniel stared at her in confusion. "What are you talking about?"

She spun away from him again, but she didn't head for the door. She began to pace in small circles next to the bed. "Really? Do you have to make me say it out loud?"

"*Christine.* Do you mind explaining what you think I'm

thinking? Because I think I'm thinking something completely different from what you think I'm thinking." He shook his own head at that linguistic nightmare, no matter how true it was.

She rolled her eyes at him. "I'm no supermodel—I never have been. I haven't lost the baby weight, either. And look at you. You're so handsome it hurts to watch you play with Marie. And you own a private jet and this condo with this view—clearly, you are richer than sin while I struggle to make rent and day care every month."

"I don't care about any of that," he put in quietly, but she ignored him.

"I'm impulsive and unnatural. I can't follow the rules and I never do the right thing. I don't even know if coming here with you was the right thing or the most spectacularly stupid thing in a long line of stupid things." She glared at him. "And you shouldn't try to make me think that you like me, that you could even like Marie. It's not fair to her." She dropped her gaze, looking defeated. "To either of us."

"He was wrong."

She jerked her head up, her eyes wide. "What?"

"Your father. He was wrong about you. If it's any consolation, he's wrong about everything, but most especially you." This time, he didn't just stroke his fingertips over her cheek. He cupped her face in his hands so she had no choice but to look at him. "You listen to me, Christine Murray. You were a teenager. All teenagers are impulsive. But that's not who you are now. I don't care what he says about you. Because the woman you are now would do anything to protect her daughter. The woman you are now is kind and thoughtful and cautious. You're the only person trying to play by the rules and if you don't let me help you, those rules will crush you. And I can't stand by and watch that happen."

He slid his hands down her shoulders and over her back, letting them settle around her waist. "I don't give a damn about the baby weight or how much you do or do not earn. I don't define your worth by your size. I define it by your actions and your actions tell me you're a woman that I could…"

That he could *what*? Trust with his own secrets? She didn't trust him and it wasn't any smarter for him to trust her.

Her eyes shone and she swallowed nervously. "Why are you saying these things to me?"

He bent his head down to meet hers. "Because I do like you."

This time, she didn't pull away. This time, he kissed her—slow and gentle at first and then, when her lips parted and welcomed him, with more heat.

Daniel had always been something of a monk. While women had always been plentiful and available, he hadn't trusted them.

In America, he was tall, dark and mysterious. In Korea, he had a hint of exoticism to him. Despite many offers, he'd taken very few lovers. When he was younger, he'd been convinced his grandfather was behind every come-on. He'd avoided dating and sex simply because he hadn't wanted to be trapped by the old man's notions of honor and duty. And then, when he began his career as a political operative, he'd gotten even more cautious, unwilling to let a one-night stand turn out to be a political liability.

So, it'd been a while. A *long* while. And when Christine sighed into his mouth and her arms came around his neck, he was almost overwhelmed by the sweetness of it all. She still tasted faintly of the ginger ale she'd drunk on the plane, but underneath that was a taste of warmth and even familiarity. He curled his fingers into her hips, pulling her closer. Her curves felt right against his chest, under his hands. He hardened as she softened against him.

Kissing Christine Murray was like finally coming home.

Then she pushed him away. Chest heaving, she closed her eyes. "Did you bring me here to seduce me?"

There was a part of him that wanted to tell her not to be so suspicious. There really weren't any ulterior motives behind the kiss, behind any of it.

But she was still Christine Murray and Daniel had to face the fact that if she was suspicious, it was because he'd made her that way.

And, just like that, they were right back to where they started. He stepped away, knowing there was nothing he could say to convince her. So he didn't. Instead, he motioned to the bed. "If you'd like to change, I had some things brought up for you. Don't worry about Marie. I'm sure my mom's having the time of her life with her. When you have the chance to…recover, we can reconvene and discuss the situation."

Her lips twisted and he couldn't tell if she was grimacing in frustration or trying not to laugh. "And which situation would *that* be?"

"Whichever situation you'd like it to be." With that, he turned and walked out.

He stopped in the kitchen to get his thoughts in order. This wasn't like him. He did not get personally involved. He did not bring people back to his apartment. And he never introduced women to his mother.

And yet, here they all were. He could hear his mom cooing with Marie and he knew that, when he went in to check on them in a few moments, his mother would ask about Christine.

Running a political campaign meant ignoring rules in favor of bigger and better stories, higher polling numbers, and victories. Especially victories. Christine hadn't been a part of her father's campaign until Daniel had made her a part of it. But he never could've predicted that it would have led to this.

Because he hadn't lied. He *did* like her. She was handling this horrible situation with a surprising amount of grace. Unlike her own father, she was fiercely loyal to her daughter. And she *was* beautiful. She was soft and curved in all the right places and she made him ache. Like right now, he thought darkly as he adjusted his trousers. He *ached* for her.

In his time, he'd lusted. But that was sex. This? This was something else.

Dimly, he was aware that she was exactly the kind of woman who would have given his grandfather an apoplectic stroke. Christine was too blonde, too blue-eyed, too outspoken and far too American to have ever satisfied Lee Dae-Won. Was that part of her appeal? Was he still trying to irritate the old man?

This should have been a simple job of salvaging a woman's reputation and shielding an infant from the media. Daniel should've manipulated the web rankings and guarded her apartment without caring for her. Hell, he could've done what he'd always done—operate behind the scenes, in secrecy, pulling the strings as he saw fit.

But he hadn't. Instead, he'd walked right into that bank of hers and made his intentions known. He'd gone to her church and flown her to Chicago and installed her in his own personal guestroom instead of a nice hotel under an assumed name. And now he had to go into the living room and watch his mother fall in love with Marie.

He had never in his life made such a mess of things and the hell of it was, even knowing it would only get messier, he wasn't sure he'd change any of it.

Because he had kissed her and because she had kissed him back and it had felt like *home*.

He grabbed a sparkling water from the fridge and went to check on his mother. She was kneeling next to the coffee table and Marie, as usual, was cruising around the edges. A plate with sliced fruit and a sippy cup half full of milk were within reach. Marie looked bright-eyed and bushy-tailed and his mother had a matching smile upon her face. She didn't even look up when he entered the room. As he removed his coat and loosened his tie, she said to him in Korean, "Is she all right?"

Daniel collapsed into a chair. Truthfully, he didn't know. "She's had a long day," he replied in Korean.

His mother slanted him a knowing look. "Did you tell her you were going to introduce her to me?"

Busted. "No..."

His mother leaned over and patted him on the knee. Marie saw this and decided to do the same, lurching toward Daniel's knees.

Minnie clucked at him. "She's been through quite a lot."

Daniel sighed heavily and caught Marie up in his arms. Marie giggled, which made him feel like he was doing something right. "She's been through a lot because of me."

Minnie came to her feet. "Did she know you were bringing her here?"

Shame heated his cheeks. His mother was the only person who could inspire this reaction in him. He had long ago learned that pissing off his grandfather was a victory and he certainly didn't give a damn what anyone else thought. But a single look from Minnie Lee and he was a misbehaving kid all over again. "I'm just trying to keep her safe. I didn't think she'd come if she knew I was bringing her here."

His mother stroked Marie's hair with such tenderness that Daniel wished he could be someone else. A more dutiful son, at least. The kind of man who would've settled down and given his mother the grandchildren she desperately wanted.

Marie obviously knew who was the soft touch in the room. She looked up at Minnie and then, grinning wildly, reached up her hands in a gesture that even Daniel knew meant she wanted to be picked up. Minnie was only too happy to oblige. She began to sing an old song in Korean, one that Daniel hadn't heard in years, *Santoki*—a song about a bunny.

Daniel thought he was off the hook, but when his mother reached the end of the first verse, she paused and looked back at him. "You have to trust her if you want her to trust you." She said it in English, which somehow made it worse.

"I do trust her," he replied, also in English. "I trusted her enough to bring her here, didn't I?"

His mother shook her head, a small gesture that still spoke loudly of her disappointment with his answer. She had never been one to bluster, like her own father had been. She was a quiet woman who lived a quiet life surrounded by fellow Korean Americans in her adopted city. Sometimes, Daniel forgot that she had been a young girl who left home and carved out a place for herself in a strange country. She had raised her son on her own, more or less. She had found her place in this world, straddling two cultures with apparent ease.

So why did he feel like he didn't belong anywhere?

"You must trust her with the truth, Dae-Hyun."

His phone chimed again—he had ignored reality for long enough. "I have some things I need to do," he said, glancing at the screen. Crap. It was Brian White. Again. Had someone connected him and Christine?

If his mother was disappointed by Daniel's announcement, she didn't show it. Instead, she said, "Don't you worry about us. Come along, Miss Marie." She began singing the bunny song again as she carried Marie over to the windows.

When they were out of earshot, Daniel answered the call. "I'm still not interested."

Brian let loose with a string of curse words. "Where the hell is she?" he finished, sputtering.

All right, so Daniel had not had the foresight to get to Marie's father first. But he had the distinct satisfaction of having pulled a fast one on Brian White.

"Who?" he asked in as innocent a voice as he could manage.

"You know goddamned well who—Christine Murray. Where is she?"

"I don't know. I would assume that she's at work?" It was a challenge to keep the humor out of his voice.

"Don't try that bullshit with me, Lee. She's disappeared off the face of the earth and I can only think of one person would have a vested interest in hiding her and that's you. So where is she?"

Daniel couldn't remember ever having this much fun. "You all right?" he asked, trying not to overdo the innocent tone. "You don't sound good."

"Answer the goddamn question. *Someone* has been burying the lede on internet stories. *Someone* has had private investigators roughing up my associates. And now *someone* has helped that girl fall off the face of the earth."

"Oh, are you talking about the Murray girl?"

Brian let loose with another string of obscenities.

"I told you I was out," Daniel said, letting anger seep into his voice.

"You better be. If I find out you're working for Rosen…"

That was it. "Is that a threat?" Because he was not going to let this man act like he still pulled the strings.

Brian must've finally recognized the warning in Daniel's tone. "Don't mess with me on this, Lee. I'm running a campaign for Clarence Murray and my employer has requested that I bring his daughter in for a chat."

"I'm skimming the search results now—it seems like someone beat you to the punch with her ex." It probably wasn't wise to pour salt into the wound, but Daniel felt a powerful need to remind Brian he was not all-knowing. "You're slipping, Brian. It's not like you."

"You're nothing but a bastard, Lee. A bastard through and through."

"Name-calling isn't very original, Brian." Even if it was true. "I'm out. I'm not working for you and I'm not working for Rosen and even if I knew where the Murray girl was, I wouldn't tell you."

"I *will* find her and I *will* bring her back into the fold. That's a promise. I just hope, for your sake, I don't find her with you."

That was most definitely a threat. In a perverse way, Daniel took pride in it. It meant that, despite the fact that he and Brian had worked together for a dozen years on political campaigns across the country, Brian had never figured out the extent of Daniel's wealth and power.

"I'll say this one more time—I'm out. But if you bother me again, I'll be back in and you won't like what happens next."

"You forget that I know your secrets," Brian sneered.

And the truth was, he probably believed that. He would be only too happy to smear Daniel's name in the press, linking him to dozens of dirty campaign tricks over the years. It might be bad press for the Beaumont Brewery— but then again, there was no such thing as bad press.

Trust her with the truth. That's what his mother had said. But she couldn't honestly mean everything. Maybe— *maybe*—Christine would understand his family history. But things like owning the majority of Lee Enterprises? He'd watched her struggle to get her mind wrapped around his plane and his condo. He'd listened to her explain in excruciating detail why she wasn't good enough for him.

He didn't know how much more truth Christine Murray could handle, frankly.

Brian, on the other hand, needed a reality check in the worst sort of way. "And I know yours. Don't make me bury you." He hung up.

He sat there, trying to look at the forest and all of the trees. He tried to envision the strings he'd need to pull to get the outcome he preferred.

But instead of mentally mapping out the playing field, his thoughts kept turning back to Christine. To the warm way her flesh had molded against his, to the sweet taste of her against his mouth. To the way he'd wanted *more*.

No. He couldn't afford to let himself get distracted now, not if Brian was already suspicious.

It was time to take this to the next level. Daniel made the call. "Natalie? When can you get to Chicago?"

Nine

This was ridiculous. Christine stared down at what was most likely several thousand dollars–worth of clothing from a department store she had never visited.

Ridiculous.

At least this time, she wasn't hiding in the ladies' room. She was hiding in the guest room. It made all the difference in the world.

She knew these were designer labels—Tahari, Calvin Klein—for pity's sake, there was even a silk Gucci top in the mix. These brands cost more than her rent for a month. Heck, even more than day care for Marie. And the bag of makeup from MAC and Chanel? In colors that would look good on her?

And it all just magically appeared because Daniel made some calls. Because Daniel liked her.

She couldn't believe that. Obviously, he had more money than she could comprehend. He owned homes in at least two countries, had his own private jet, and this condo was the kind of place that didn't come cheap. Just like the clothing.

She touched the Gucci top, letting the cool silk slip over her fingers. The tags had all been removed, but she was willing to bet this top alone was worth at least five hundred dollars, maybe more.

In other words, it was not the kind of top a dumpy single mom wore. Marie would destroy this thing within seconds, if not sooner.

Christine should've been more specific when she had given Daniel her clothing size. She should have said some yoga pants and T-shirts would've been fine. That's what she would've packed, if she had gone home.

But even as she thought that, she cringed. Would she really have sat around in this glamorous condominium with this glamorous view next to this glamorous man in her decidedly nonglamorous yoga pants?

What the heck. If he'd paid for these clothes, she'd wear them. And Marie would destroy them, of that she had no doubt. But for at least five minutes she would pretend that she fit into Daniel's world.

She fixed her face—and danged if her skin didn't look amazingly dewy with those high-end cosmetics. Then she slid the silk shirt on and was pleased to see her boobs looked great. The pair of embellished dark-wash jeans slid on like second skin. There was even a thick chocolate brown cardigan because, after all, March in Chicago was not any warmer than March in Denver.

She eyed the long flannel nightgown with matching robe. Oscar de la Renta. Even the nightie was designer.

She didn't know how she would go out there and look at him—or his mother. He had kissed her and she had kissed him back. For a little while, anyway.

What if she were wrong? What if she were looking for a

deeper meaning here and there just wasn't one? Could she seriously take Daniel at his word? She wanted to. Desperately, she wanted to. But every time she felt herself being swayed by his thoughtfulness, by the way he played with Marie—by the way he touched Christine, like she was a delicate thing to be treasured—she would remember the truth of the situation.

She'd gotten pregnant out of wedlock. But he'd made it national news.

So she was wearing designer clothes. That didn't mean she trusted him. It didn't mean she wanted him to kiss her again. She didn't want it and she didn't need it.

Yeah, right.

From somewhere inside this cavernous apartment, she heard Marie giggling and a soft feminine voice responding. Everything seemed fine, just as he'd promised it would be.

And that was another thing. He hadn't told her where they were going—other than the generic *Chicago*. He hadn't told her that his mother would be here. Not that Christine was complaining about that. Luxury was not only wearing designer clothes, but it was having half an hour to wash her face and get dressed.

It was all so different from her normal life. She pressed the palms of her hands into her temples, trying to get her head to stop spinning.

"Are you all right?"

Christine let out a little gasp. Daniel had appeared out of nowhere to stand in front of her, worry etched on his face. She was instantly aware of him on a different level. A physical level.

"Oh, fine," she said, trying to sound nonchalant and failing miserably. "Everything about this is fine."

His suit jacket and tie were gone and he had unbuttoned

the top two buttons on his pristine white dress shirt. He had even cuffed the sleeves, revealing forearms that were far more muscular than she expected.

Her gaze slid over the V of his waist. Without the jacket—or the bulky cable-knit sweater he'd worn to church—she could see the shape of his legs. And he had taken off his shoes! Instead of basic socks that matched his gray trousers, he wore socks with wildly colorful paisleys. She felt like she should have noticed those socks earlier.

"Yes, I can tell." Daniel's gaze swept over her, warming her from the inside out. "I see the clothes worked. That top suits you perfectly."

Christine could feel her cheeks burning up at his leisurely perusal of her person. "It really wasn't necessary to spend that much money on clothes Marie is going to destroy, you know."

"It was worth it."

All of her warm feelings took a hard right into embarrassment. Why did he keep doing this? Was it because of the kiss? "Stop."

His gaze hardened as he took another step closer. "Why can't you take a compliment?"

Instinctively, she took a step back, which brought her up hard against the countertop. "What?"

"You are a lovely woman and the clothing looks nice on you. I'm trying to compliment you. Not because I'm trying to seduce you and not because I want something out of you." His eyes glittered with emotion that she was afraid to identify. Lust? Anger? "I like you and I am expressing that in a commonly accepted form. Stop tearing yourself down. You look *nice*," he said, leaning in. Less than a foot separated them now. When Christine couldn't come up with a response, he added with an amused grin, "This is the part where you say *thank you*."

She blinked hard, tears stinging her eyes and she wasn't sure why. "Thank you. The clothes are lovely."

"Closer," he murmured, putting a hand on the counter on either side of her. She was trapped and that was maybe a bad thing but she desperately wanted it to be good.

Her body pulsed with need and this time, that need wouldn't be ignored. Especially not when Daniel said, "The clothes are lovely because *you* make them lovely, Christine."

She wasn't strong enough, darn it all. "You're trying to make me like you." He moved closer and she put a hand on his chest. It was the first time she'd touched him and, through the fine cotton of his shirt, she could feel the warmth of his body.

In another life, she'd do more than just rest her palm against his chest. The old Christine would still be in the back bedroom with him. The old Christine would've thrown herself into that kiss because he truly was her knight in shining armor—well, her knight in a suit, anyway.

But the new woman she was didn't do that. She didn't even slide her hand around his waist or pull him in until her breasts were flush against his chest. She just…touched him. It shouldn't have been a big deal, that touch.

But it was.

His eyes darkened. "I'd like to think I don't have to try that hard." Smoothly, he pushed off the counter and put more space between them. He did so in a way that kept her hand from dropping away from his chest. She wasn't pushing him, but she wasn't breaking the contact, either. "There's something about you…" he said, his voice trailing off as he leaned into her touch.

Please say the right thing—something she could believe in.

"But," he said, going on in a more formal voice, "I understand if you don't feel the same way after what I did to you two years ago."

She let her hand fall away as she opened her mouth to try and make sense of the confusion. But at that moment, Marie let out a familiar shriek of, "Mama!"

"Oh," Christine said dully. "I need to check on her."

She went to step around him, but he put a hand on her waist, stopping her when she was parallel with him. God, he was so hot—heat radiated from his side, where it was pressed against hers. "Maybe we can talk tonight?"

She should say no. She shouldn't believe anything he said at this point or at any other point. She shouldn't agree to being alone with him, especially not under cover of darkness. It was too risky and there was too much at stake. This was all happening far too fast.

But he was looking down at her with those beautiful eyes. He liked her. He had already kissed her. He wasn't working for her father and she didn't think he was working for the opposition.

She had tried to be good for two years and what had it gotten her? Hounded by the press and dragged through the mud. Again. Maybe she didn't want to be good anymore. That had to be the reason she lifted her hand and stroked it over his smooth cheek.

"Okay," she said in a soft voice. "Tonight, we'll talk."

Then she slipped out of his grasp and went to check on her daughter.

Daniel had a feast of Korean food delivered and opened a good bottle of wine. Christine didn't even have to clean up—she offered, but he waved her away. He stacked the dishes and threw away the take-out boxes, but he said he had a maid who cleaned up for him. Then Minnie swept Marie up and declared that the child needed a bath.

All in all, it was one of the nicer evenings Christine had had in a long time. She sent a text to Sue at the bank, assuring her that Christine was all right. She called Mrs. McDonald, too. She sent a message to her boss, explaining that she'd be back to work in a few days and apologizing for the whole mess.

Between the low-pressure meal and the wine, Christine was able to relax—something she didn't really allow herself to do anymore. She rarely drank because she was always the responsible parent on duty.

Far removed from the reporters and the daily struggle of caring for her daughter, Christine began to think of this interlude as a vacation. After all, she was staying with a gorgeous man who provided child care and all accommodations—while looking at her with desire in his eyes.

Sooner or later, she would to go back to her decent job at the bank and her daily struggle to get Marie to bed early so Christine could have fifteen minutes to herself before she collapsed from exhaustion.

She wanted to enjoy this. More than that, she wanted to enjoy it without having to pay for it later. That was the sticking point. Would all this come back to haunt her tomorrow? That was the question she had to ask as Daniel came to sit beside her on his massive couch. It stretched out for almost fifteen feet—far larger than any regular couch. And it faced the floor-to-ceiling windows that looked out over Lake Michigan. Even as dusk faded into night, the view was amazing.

"She's in love with that baby," Daniel said as Minnie carried a squirming Marie, wrapped in a fluffy towel that looked like a duck, into the living room so Christine could see how good her daughter had been. Then they were off again, Minnie singing Korean lullabies and armed with a small stack of brand-new children's books.

"I picked up on that, it's true." There were cookie crumbs on the coffee table and random toys scattered all over the place, but he didn't seem to mind. Minnie and Daniel cared about Marie.

God, how Christine needed more of that in her life.

To her horror, she heard herself ask, "How come you're not married? You know your mom would adore grand-children."

After a long pause, Daniel said, "We need to talk a little business," in a voice that was regretful. "If you're up to it."

"All right." *Business* seemed like a nice way of saying the complete and total collapse of her life. *Business*, she repeated to herself several more times.

She'd like some more wine before they got down to *business*, but she hadn't nursed Marie yet. She needed the closeness with her daughter, the one single thing that was a familiar part of their routine.

"Natalie Wesley will be here tomorrow evening," Daniel announced into the silence.

"She will?" Christine wasn't normally the kind to get starstruck but… "Why?"

"I'd like her to conduct a sit-down interview with you where we're in complete control of the conversation."

Okay, her heart was definitely pounding. "Is that a good idea?"

The apartment was dark, with only a few lamps lit at the far ends of the couch. Christine could see, but she felt less exposed.

Then Daniel reached over and curled his fingers around hers. It wasn't the same kind of touch that had led to the kiss earlier—but it still sent sparks of electricity over her skin. "You can't hide forever, Christine, as nice as it might be for all of us." She swung her head around at that statement but Daniel went on in a gentle voice, "It's better to control your narrative than to let someone else control it. You have to tell your own story."

Hadn't that been the problem the last time? He'd defined her first. "Do I have to?"

"Absolutely not." He squeezed her fingers and then slid his hand around so they were palm to palm. "But Natalie and I agree that it's a good idea. I promise she won't ask any gotcha-style questions. She's working up the questions and answers now."

"The answers? Good Lord, you don't leave anything to chance, do you?"

He chuckled, a rich sound that surrounded her. "I try not to. I don't mean that she'll have a script for you to read from—that wouldn't be believable. It'll be more like talking points."

She mulled that over—while also trying to figure out if she wanted to pull her hand away or not.

She didn't want to. His hand was warm and heavy, almost a promise of good things to come. She felt safe with him. She had all along, she had to admit. Because if she hadn't, she wouldn't have met him in the church, wouldn't have let Marie grow attached to him and she certainly wouldn't have let him whisk them away.

She trusted him. If that made her a fool, then, she was a fool. She gave his hand a little squeeze. "Like... I wish my father all the luck in his campaign but I'm far too busy raising my daughter to join him on the campaign trail?"

He turned to look at her, warmth in his eyes. "Yes," he murmured, the space between them closing, "exactly like that."

He was going to kiss her again and she was going to let him. This time, she was going to enjoy it, by God.

"Here we are," Minnie's chipper voice announced seconds before she came back into the living room with Marie curled against her shoulder. "It's bedtime for a sleepy little girl, isn't it, sweetheart?" She sighed and kissed the top of Marie's head. "And I need to head home."

Christine and Daniel both jerked back like they were teenagers caught kissing by, well, his mother. "I'll call the car for you, Mom," Daniel said, looking completely unflustered while Christine knew her face was burning.

She stood. "I usually nurse her at night," she said, holding out her arms. Marie leaned toward her and Christine let her daughter's heavy body ground her in reality. "If you'll excuse us. Minnie, thank you so, so much. This has been a wonderful evening. Will we get to see you again before we go back to Denver?"

"Oh, I hope so." The older woman's eyes lit up. "I have something to do tomorrow morning but I'd love to come back over in the afternoon?" She looked longingly at Marie and Christine knew she hadn't been wrong. Minnie Lee had grandbabies on the brain. "You two could go out, do something fun. Miss Marie and I will be just fine."

Daniel cleared his throat and, finally, he looked embarrassed. "Mom, that's not a smart idea right now. We're trying to keep Christine out of the public eye. But," he went on before his mother could respond, "Natalie will be here tomorrow evening to interview Christine and it'd be a huge help if you could entertain Marie for us during that." He turned to Christine. "Wouldn't it?"

She would have sworn there was a hint of pleading in his tone, a need to keep his mother happy. "It would be wonderful," she agreed, patting Marie's back.

Minnie clapped her hands. "Is three okay? I could cut one meeting short…"

"No," Christine said quickly, "three is fine. She'll probably be waking up from her nap by then."

"Wonderful." Minnie moved as if she wanted to hug Marie—and, by extension, Christine—before pulling to a stop. "Tomorrow, then."

Christine nodded and carried Marie back to where the portable crib had been set up. That man had even had a glider delivered. Everything she needed had appeared out of thin air. Clothes, food—compliments. Sincere, dangerous compliments.

He was, in a word, perfect.

God, she hoped she wasn't about to make a fool of herself.

Ten

"I'm exhausted. I might just turn in," Christine said, already moving down the hall.

Of course she was. It'd been a day. But that didn't make him any less disappointed that she wouldn't be back out—where they would finally be alone. "That's fine. Get some sleep."

The moment Christine was out of earshot, his mother rounded on him. "Dae-Hyun," she said, using his Korean name and that particular tone of voice that made him feel like he was six. "Why haven't you told her?"

"About what?"

They both knew what. His mother shook her head and Daniel had to force back the uncomfortable feeling that he had disappointed her. "About you. Does she know who you really are?"

If he had less self-discipline, he'd throw his hands up in frustration. But he had a lot of self-discipline. "That's not some deep mystery, Mom. I'm the former political campaign operative who ruined her life."

If there were one person in the whole world he couldn't fool, though, it was his mother. Only Minnie could cut through the crap with one well-placed look. With a sigh of resignation, she stepped closer and patted him on the cheek. "There is more to you than that. And more to her than just a woman whose life you ruined." Her eyes twinkled. "She's the first woman you've ever shown your home to—as far as I know," she said before Daniel could say the exact same thing. "You can't tell me that's just because you're trying to make up for what happened before."

He wasn't going to win an argument with his mother. Especially not when there was a distinctive chance she was right. So Daniel leaned down and kissed his mom on the cheek. "Thanks for your help today. We'll see you tomorrow?"

She notched an eyebrow at him. "You can't avoid the truth forever, you know," she said softly in Korean. Then she went to get her things.

He saw her out. He wasn't avoiding anything. He *wasn't*. He was a full-grown man who was helping to manage one business and keeping tabs on another. He ran his business interests and protected his family members. He...

He'd never brought a woman back to his place. The few times he had taken a lover—he was no saint—he had arranged for five-star hotels.

Damn it, he hated it when his mother could see right through him.

Because there hadn't been a single good reason to bring Christine back here. He could have gotten her a penthouse suite and had all the clothes and things for her daughter delivered there. He could have stayed there as well, if that was what she'd been comfortable with.

But that's not what he'd done. He'd brought her straight here, straight to his mother.

What had he done?

What made it worse was the fact that he wanted to talk to Christine tonight. He wanted reassurances that she was okay with what was happening. He wanted to know that...

Well, that she didn't hate him. He was willing to accept that she didn't like him, that she might not ever like him. But in some perverse way, he wanted to make sure he was making things better instead of worse.

He wanted to know he wasn't failing her. That's really what it came down to.

He wasn't going to find out tonight—whether she liked him, whether she wanted him to kiss her again. He wanted to kiss her again, he had to admit to himself as he sat down on the couch and refilled his wineglass. She'd barely had a glass and he hated to see a good bottle go to waste.

She was a little right, he thought halfway through the glass. She wasn't his type. Did he *have* a type? The few women he'd had affairs with had some things in common. They hadn't been looking for a relationship any more than Daniel had. They had wanted certain needs fulfilled to their satisfaction—discreetly. There hadn't been a common look, despite what Christine seemed to think. He'd simply wanted his affairs to be casual and easy.

There was nothing casual or easy about Christine Murray. Not only did she have more baggage than the average woman, she had more skin in the game. She had Marie.

It should have sent him running. The man he'd been when his grandfather had been alive would have put as much distance between himself and Christine as physically possible.

So why hadn't he? She kept asking him that same question—why was he doing this?

He knew he hadn't answered Christine's questions. And the truth was, he didn't have answers. He didn't know why he was inserting himself into her life. He didn't know why, for the first time in his life, he cared.

Except that he felt the pull to protect her. That was how it had started. He had wanted to make things right. And then he had seen her daughter and he'd wanted to protect the little girl. And through it all, no matter what curveball he threw at her, Christine kept herself together with grace and dignity. She might be the strongest woman he'd ever met.

His mother had suggested she could watch Marie while he and Christine went out and did something fun and he'd shot her down. But why couldn't they? The odds of Christine being recognized in Chicago were slim and the odds of Marie being recognized were so small as to be laughable. There were two pictures of her on the internet, neither of them great.

With a few precautions, they should be able to go out. He found himself looking down to where Navy Pier was lit up. The whole front of the Pier was a gigantic children's museum—the kind where kids could play and parents could watch or join in.

In the reflection of the glass, he saw the light in the hall flick on behind him, saw Christine silhouetted in the doorway. He turned, feeling ridiculously hopeful. She'd come back out and damned if she didn't look like an angel, backlit by the hall light. The gold in her hair and the white robe, with the silhouette of her body just hinted at…

She simply took his breath away. That ache came back and it took everything he had not to stride over to her and pull her into his arms and pick up where that earlier kiss had left off. And this time, he didn't want to stop.

He didn't move.

"Oh," she said, twisting her hands in the belt of the bathrobe. "I didn't know you were still up."

"I was just thinking." Not strategizing, not working—just thinking. About her. "Is everything all right?"

She dropped her hands to her sides. "I wanted a cup of tea. I didn't mean to disturb you."

He moved toward the kitchen and was gratified when she followed him. He filled the electric kettle. "Chamomile?"

He set the tea caddy before her and tried not to stare. He hadn't specified what kind of clothing he'd wanted for her. He had merely called in her size, her coloring and what he thought she might need for an extended visit. The personal shoppers had done everything else—and they had done their job well. The nightgown was long, brushing the tops of her toes. It was awfully modest, a heavyweight cotton flannel, maybe. And a matching robe had come with it. She was, in essence, covered from head to toe. She shouldn't have looked sensual. She should have looked like she was wrapped in a sheet.

But even that thought spiraled another set of images through his mind, ones of her wearing his sheet and nothing else. Nothing except a smile—that he'd put there.

He couldn't read the look on her face—was it confusion or amusement? "Every time I think I have you figured out, you throw me for another loop."

He frowned, leaning on the counter. "How so?"

She looked down at the gown and robe. "When a man buys a woman a nightgown, it rarely involves this much fabric."

And he remembered her asking if he had planned on seducing her. "I wanted you to be warm."

He thought she blushed. "I am."

He might have had too much wine because suddenly

he couldn't fight it any longer. He had to hold her, feel the weight of her body against his. He pulled her into his arms. A miracle occurred—she let him. Her arms came around his waist and she nuzzled against him. She was soft and warm and he closed his eyes and inhaled deeply.

"Christine…" he said softly, against her hair. He wanted to say so much but for once in his life, he didn't know how.

She did this to him, turned him inside out and upside down. She made him ache for her, for a glimpse of a man that he'd be in another life. A man she trusted. A man she *wanted*. Because he wanted her. He couldn't ignore it any longer.

"Don't talk," she said in a voice that he felt more than heard. "Just…don't."

So he didn't. Instead, he held her as tightly as he could, letting his body take some of the weight off her shoulders. Her breasts were barely contained by the fabric and they pressed against his chest with each breath she took. And him? His blood was pounding in his veins and that physical ache had focused where she was touching him, making him hard.

But he was oddly happy anyway. There was an intimacy to this that he didn't want to take for granted. He couldn't remember the last time he had held a woman like this.

The kettle clicked, jarring them out of the moment. Reluctantly—at least, Daniel hoped it was reluctantly—Christine pulled away from him. But she stayed within the space between his legs and his hands settled on her hips. He'd slid down against the counter so far that he could almost look her in the eye. Her face was nearly lost in the shadows, but she was staring at him. He could feel it.

"My bedroom's on the far side of the condo," he said in a quiet voice. "If you need anything at all, don't hesitate to come get me."

He meant it sincerely. But it was only after her eyes widened slightly that he realized there was an additional meaning to his words. Damn it.

But then she said, "I won't."

He wanted to kiss her—he wanted so much from her. But he didn't want to put her in a position where she felt trapped.

Yet he couldn't *not* touch her. So instead, he cupped her face and kissed her forehead. Heat flooded his body, a raw physical reaction that wasn't something he'd planned for.

He made himself break the contact. He'd had wine and she'd had a terrible day and the fastest way to make sure she didn't trust him would be to seduce her.

So he was shocked when, after he pulled away, she leaned up on her toes and pressed her lips against his.

If he'd ached before, the lust that roared through his body now was just shy of sheer pain. Desire hit him low and hard. There was a hunger to her mouth that set his blood humming and made him dizzy. The kiss was far sweeter than the one he had taken earlier because Christine gave it to him. She'd come to his arms. She'd kissed him.

He didn't want to be noble. He wanted to take and give—especially give. He wanted to peel Christine out of this nightgown and lay her out on his bed and kiss every single inch of her luscious body. He slid his hands down her waist, cupping her bottom and pulling her against his erection.

Which was a mistake. Too much, too fast. She rocked back on her heels, her chest heaving. He caught her around the waist. "We…we can't."

He didn't let go of her. He wasn't sure he could even if he wanted to. Instead, he dug his fingertips into her skin. "We can't?"

"I…" she took a deep breath—but she hadn't stepped

clear of him yet. "I can't make another mistake," she told him in a whisper, her voice shaking. "I can't be hurt again."

It damn near broke his heart to hear that, to know he was the reason for that pain. "I won't hurt you. Not ever again."

"How can I believe you?" Her voice was stronger, suddenly—an edge to it.

"Let me show you, babe." He pulled her into another kiss, rougher this time. She melted into him, a small sound of need coming from high in her throat. "Let me take care of you."

He could do that for her. Put her first. Let her call the shots while he took care of everything else.

"Daniel," she whispered against his mouth as her arms went around his neck.

Yes. Her body was flush against his, the delicious weight of her breasts pressing against his chest. He ran his hands up and down her back, squeezing her bottom again, harder this time. "Tell me what you want, babe," he asked as he brushed kisses over her cheeks, her forehead, her lips.

Because what he wanted was to pick her up and carry her back to his bed. Or the couch. Hell, he'd settle for laying her out on the damned dining room table—anywhere was fine, as long as he could make her cry out with pleasure. But he wouldn't do anything without her permission. He wanted her to trust that, deep down, he wanted her. This wasn't because she was convenient and available. Nothing about her was convenient, was it?

She gripped his head between her hands. In the dim light, she looked like an avenging angel, come down to earth to mete out the punishment for his sins. "I don't want to regret this." Oh, yeah—she was definitely angry now.

He deserved that anger. He honestly didn't even know how she could want him. But she did because even as she said it, she hitched one of her legs up as high as the nightgown would allow and wrapped it around his leg. He could feel the tantalizing heat of her, so close to his throbbing erection. "I don't want to regret you, Daniel." It was an order.

One he'd follow if it killed him. "God help me, you won't." He lifted her against him, his hips already moving against her. She gasped as he thrust against her, so close but yet so far away. "I promise, Christine—you won't." He pushed himself away from the counter, lifting her as he stood. "Yes?"

She hesitated, but only for a second. "Yes."

He wanted to shout with an excitement he hadn't felt in a long time. Holding her up, her legs around his hips and her mouth against his, he kissed her with a passion so intense he barely recognized it.

She pulled away. "I shouldn't like you, damn it. Start walking."

Had he ever heard her curse before? "But you do, anyway."

"You ruined everything," she whispered, and then her lips fastened on to his neck, moving down until she was below the collar of his shirt. "Everything," she repeated. Then she bit him.

A spike of pain and pleasure jerked his dick to attention. He groaned as she sucked at his neck, punishing him and rewarding him all at the same time.

"Are you going to make me pay for it?" He couldn't walk with this hard-on, couldn't carry her while she was taking all of her frustrations out on him. He collapsed onto the couch.

She straddled him and he hiked her nightgown up to her

hips. "Yes," she hissed before crushing her mouth down onto his. He tried to pull the nightgown up even farther—off would be great—but she grabbed his hands and pinned them against the back of the couch.

She was fierce, his Christine, holding him down and taking what she wanted. He could have pulled free, rolled her onto her back and taken her—but this wasn't about him. This was about her—her life, her taking control.

So he let her exact her revenge one bruising kiss at a time. He'd never had angry sex before. His affairs had always been detached, almost, focused on the physical with as little emotion as possible.

But this? Christine grinding down on his erection, holding him by the wrists and nipping at his lower lip while her breasts rubbed against his chest?

This was all about the emotion.

"I don't like you," she whispered fiercely as she pushed herself up and let go of his wrists. "I don't."

He heard the lie in her voice and felt it in her hands as she jerked the fly of his pants open. He wouldn't have thought he could get any harder—but this thing between them—it wasn't like anything he'd ever felt before.

The fact that she made him feel at all—it was something. Did she even realize that? "I want you so bad," he groaned again as her fingertips stroked over him through his boxer briefs.

"Stop talking." She yanked his pants down a little and shoved his briefs aside. "Just stop talking, Daniel. I had to change who I was because of you—" she stroked him once, "and move to a new place." She rose over him again and positioned him at her entrance. "I had to leave behind my friends and my job and—" She bore down on him and he slid up into her in one hard thrust. "Oh, God," she moaned.

"Christine," he got out through gritted teeth. She was hot and wet and tight around him, gripping him with such urgency that he almost came right then and there.

He cupped her breasts in his hands, trying to figure out how to get to her skin. Her body and the way she was surrounding him was all he could see and feel and think. But it wasn't enough. He needed more. God, he'd never needed more in his life.

"No." For a split second, he thought she'd changed her mind and a part of him nearly died. But instead of throwing herself off him, she grabbed his hands and held them against the back of the couch. "I'm doing this, Daniel." With that, she began to rise and fall.

"You're in charge," he managed to say before his mind quit trying to think. "That's it. Ride me. Ride me hard."

"Shut up." Her mouth crushed down onto his again with such savage fury that he knew he was going to be bruised and he didn't care.

He took it all—all of her rage, her lust, her burdens. He took everything she had to give him. He thrust up into her and, when her head fell back with a low moan, he leaned forward and dragged his teeth over the layers of flannel, biting and sucking until he had one of her nipples hard and pointed. He nipped at her again until she released one wrist and, threading her fingers through his hair, shoved his head back. "You do that again and I'll stop."

That noise—needy, almost a whimper—that wasn't him, was it? It was. She'd reduced him to this—and God help him, he liked it.

He did what he could—thrusting up into her with a steady rhythm, rolling with her when she shifted from side to side. He let her chase her orgasm at her own speed. It was hers to take.

Still, his control started to fray as she rode him. She

felt so good that, although he needed to come, he didn't want to. He didn't want this to end.

"Daniel," she moaned, falling and rising faster and faster. "Oh—*Daniel.*"

"Yeah," he said, encouraging her. "You feel so good."

"Shh," she hissed before grinding down on him.

Daniel felt her body tighten, heard the noises of desire from high in the back of her throat. "Take it, Christine," he said as her grip on his hands tightened.

And then he couldn't hold back. As her body held his in the throes of her climax, his control slipped and he came with her.

She collapsed onto his shoulder, panting heavily. Her arms went around his neck and his went around her waist and they were right back to where they'd started in the kitchen—except it was more intimate now because he was still inside of her.

His head began to clear from the fog of lust—and that wasn't necessarily a good thing.

He'd just had sex with Christine.

On the couch. Without a condom.

In his condo.

Where he'd never even brought a woman home before.

And then it only got worse because Christine pushed off him and then completely off the couch. She stood while the hem of her nightgown floated back down to her feet and then, before Daniel could do anything, *say* anything, she whispered, "Good night," and moved away from him.

He hadn't even been able to come up with a reasonable compliment, for God's sake.

She had taken everything he had.

Turnabout was fair play, it seemed.

Eleven

After tossing and turning most of the night—plus getting up with Marie at two—Christine wasn't feeling as fresh as a daisy when she dragged herself out of bed.

Last night, she had kissed Daniel. And slept with him.

Well, there hadn't been a lot of actual sleeping. That was a dodge on the truth and the truth was…

She'd had sex with Daniel. Raw, hard, desperate, *angry* sex. Because she'd been furious with him for putting her in the spotlight two years ago, angry that she was back in the spotlight. But under that anger, the sparks of attraction were too hot to ignore.

Lord, it'd been amazing. It'd been two years since she'd had sex—but she didn't remember it being that electric—or intense. She shivered thinking about the climax that had ripped through her.

However, once again, that physical act hadn't brought clarity. If anything, she was more confused now than ever.

Because she'd had sex with Daniel. It was exactly the

same kind of impulsive, careless act that had gotten her here. Except now, the potential for blowback was even more dangerous because of Marie.

Christine's baby girl was still asleep in her crib and Christine needed a shower. There was no way she was going to face Daniel with yesterday's deodorant under her armpits.

The bathroom was outfitted with all the luxuries she never got to enjoy. The shampoo was the finest. The soap was the finest. The conditioner was the finest. The lotion was the finest. The towels—good Lord, she could write poetry about the towels. They were heated.

She showered and shaved and dried off, telling herself she wasn't getting all pretty for Daniel and knowing that was a lie. She cracked open the bathroom door but didn't hear any sounds from Marie, so she closed it again and found a blow dryer.

When she had her hair looking decent, she pulled the robe back on and went to the guest room. She found a tank top, along with a pale peach tunic shirt and another cardigan, this one longer and a soft gray. There was even a pair of riding boots—real leather. And the crazy thing was, it all fit. She tucked the jeans into the boots and zipped them up, the calf just making it closed.

Layers were good. Layers would hide her lumps and stretch marks. Layers would protect her from Daniel's intense gazes.

Another lie. Because the layers of nightgown and robe last night hadn't done a darned thing to slow them down.

Doyle had been gone by the time she was six months pregnant. But the two months between finding out she was pregnant and Doyle bailing on her had not been a time of great intimacy and togetherness. The moment she'd become a news story, Doyle had started putting space between them. In public, he had stood by her side and held her hand—but in private...

They'd barely spoken. She'd been with him and yet *not* with him at the same time and she had known long before she had come home to the empty apartment that she had lost him.

She'd been alone since then—but she was too drained at the end of the day to feel sorry for herself. Self-pity was a luxury she simply didn't have the time or energy for. And in all honesty, she hadn't missed the sex. Well, she'd missed the crazy sex she and Doyle had had when they'd first hooked up. But not the lifeless going-through-the-motions sex that had marked their last months as a couple.

But last night, Daniel holding her like she meant something to him—she hadn't felt completely alone in the world.

That was all it took to make her revert back to her wild ways, apparently. Five minutes in the kitchen and she'd all but dragged him to his couch and had her way with him. For Pete's sake, they hadn't even made it to a bed. They hadn't even gotten undressed.

And now she had to go out there and face him, wearing clothes he had purchased for her. He would probably try and tell her how nice she looked again and she would struggle to accept a compliment.

She listened hard, but couldn't hear any fussing from Marie. If Christine was going to face this man, it was going to involve under-eye concealer.

Finally, dressed and ready for whatever the day held— she didn't even want to think about the possibilities—she tiptoed into Marie's room.

Only to find that the crib was empty.

Oh, crap. She flew out of the bedroom, torn between

stark panic and the logical explanation that Marie couldn't have gotten out of the apartment and probably hadn't done anything as deadly as stick a fork in an electrical outlet.

Christine skidded into the living room and came to a dead halt when she saw Daniel, sprawled out on the couch, Marie resting on his chest. A thick throw was tucked around them and in one hand, Daniel held a book. The other rested on Marie's stomach, keeping her from rolling off.

Marie was telling him the story and he was listening.

Oh, it simply wasn't *fair* how perfect he was. Never mind the fact that Christine hadn't had a date in twenty months. Never mind the fact that she might not have another date for another twenty months, if ever.

Daniel Lee was in the process of ruining her for any other man. He was too handsome, too rich, too good at sex—but that wasn't the issue. No, the thing that was going to be the death of her was the way he held her as if she was precious to him, the way he was saying, "Oh, really?" every time Marie looked up at him.

He was taking care of her and her daughter and Christine wasn't an idiot. She knew exactly how rare both of those things were.

No one else would ever meet this impossibly high bar that Daniel Lee was setting. If she weren't careful, he would make her fall in love with him and then where would she be?

He looked up, his gaze meeting hers and she could feel his mouth against hers, feel the hard planes of his body pressing into hers. She could feel the physical pain of loneliness all over again and it scared her because she knew what would happen if she let that rule her. She'd spent a good six years chasing away that loneliness and she had been paying the price for it since.

So it was settled. She was absolutely not going to fall in love with Daniel Lee.

"Good morning," he said in his silky voice. He looked rumpled, his hair mussed from where she'd driven her fingers through it.

She swallowed hard, trying to remember who she'd been before she'd straddled him. On this very couch.

Hell. At least he and Marie were sitting on the far side, a good ten feet from what had happened last night. "Good morning. How is everyone today?"

Marie looked up at her, grinning wildly. Christine could tell that her daughter was still a little fuzzy from sleep, her hair sticking out wildly on all sides. But the baby made no move for Christine to pick her up from Daniel's chest. If anything, Marie seemed to burrow deeper.

A sound came from the kitchen behind her and she jumped in surprise. "Don't worry," Daniel said quickly. "It's only the maid."

She blinked at him. "Oh, of course. Only the maid."

He slanted a smile in her direction and then, without breaking eye contact, leaned down and kissed the top of Marie's head. "Sunny has some coffee going and she's making breakfast, if you're interested."

"Coffee would be good." It would be *great*. She needed something to help her make sense of this world she found herself in. She felt a little like Alice having stumbled through the looking glass, where nothing made sense.

Sunny, it turned out, was a young Korean woman and she was pulling a pan of fresh-baked muffins out of the oven. She nodded shyly at Christine.

"Thank you," Christine said as the smell of the muffins—blueberry?—hit her nose. "Is there coffee?"

The young woman crinkled her eyes as if she didn't understand completely, but she pointed at the coffeepot and Christine nodded, hoping she was being encouraging and not patronizing. "Yes, thank you."

Strangely, the maid's presence reassured Christine. With another person in the apartment, she didn't think there'd be awkwardness about what had happened last night.

Sex. Angry sex. *Great* angry sex.

"I need to talk to you," Daniel said right in her ear.

She spun around, nearly clocking Marie upside her head. "What?"

Daniel said something in Korean to Sunny, who smiled and bobbed her head as she rushed forward to lift Marie from Daniel's arms and carry her over to the high chair.

Daniel slid his hand under Christine's arm and pulled her close to the windows. "About last night…"

"Do you have to make this awkward?" Although, given the way his thumb was rubbing little circles on the inside of her elbow and given the way she wanted to do nothing more than throw herself at him again, it appeared there wasn't any way to make this *not* awkward. "Or are you going to throw this back in my face as concrete proof that you were right about me two years ago?"

His face hardened and he said in a low voice, "Yes, I have to make this awkward. We didn't use a condom."

Flames licked up the side of her face—that's how hot her cheeks burned. "Oh." She dropped her gaze to where he was still holding on to her and his hand fell away. "Don't worry about it."

"I think I'm entitled to worry about it. What if, Christine?" he asked, which was both touching, that he cared whether or not he got her pregnant, and infuriating all the same and she didn't know why.

Of course he didn't want to get her pregnant. Because if he did, he'd be tied to her forever, his name dragged through the mud with hers. Another baby would simply be another problem to manage.

"I have an IUD. I can't get pregnant," she blurted out. Daniel's eyebrows shot up at this, so Christine lowered her voice. "I had one put in after Marie was born. I couldn't risk another surprise pregnancy. Which is funny, since last night was the first time I've had sex in..."

Her voice trailed off because she made the mistake of looking up at him. Instead of shocked or angry, his mouth had curved up on one side. Was he smiling? At her?

Darn his hide. "So don't worry about it," she whispered angrily, stepping around him and heading back to where Marie was banging on the high chair tray.

In short order, Christine had eggs, bacon and fresh blueberry muffins to go with some of the best coffee she had ever had in her life. Daniel followed her to the table and they sat down to eat as if this were an everyday occurrence.

Was this just how it was going to be? Everything was the best when it came to Daniel. The best food, the best clothes, the best apartment—and who could forget the best sex?

She exhaled heavily, trying not to be angry at Daniel or at the situation or at life, in general. She wasn't sure she was making it, though. Last night, she'd done something selfish. And wonderful. Was it wrong if she didn't want to face any fallout from that?

As Marie made headway into destroying her muffin, Christine decided to cut straight to the chitchat. "So, what are we doing today? Just hanging out here?" It would be peaceful and quiet and there was a lot to be said for that right now.

"We can," Daniel replied. "But we have another option.

If you want to, there's the Chicago Children's Museum down at the Pier. We could take Marie."

Christine gaped at him, wondering if she really had fallen through the looking glass. "Didn't you tell your mother that we were trying to lie low last night? I didn't hallucinate that, did I?"

He shrugged, looking completely innocent. It didn't look right on him. "It's one of those big areas with lots of fun things. It'll be crowded and noisy on a cold day like today. Everyone's going to be paying attention to their kids—not to each other. But we can stay in if you'd like. Natalie won't get here until about six tonight."

She looked out the expansive floor-to-ceiling windows where the maid was now wiping Marie's fingerprints off everything. If they stayed in all day, her daughter would continue to destroy this pristine apartment. But if they went to a children's museum...

"You don't think we'll get caught?" She winced at how juvenile she sounded.

But he didn't react as if she had said something dumb. "We didn't get caught at your church—and those were people who knew who you were. I think you're relatively safe here." She must've frowned or something because he added, "If I didn't think it was safe, I wouldn't suggest it. It'll be fun."

She eyed him. "You don't strike me as the kind of guy who has a lot of fun."

Something in his gaze shifted, sending tingles of electricity racing down her back. "I know how to have a good time." His voice came out husky and deep and her body responded.

Oh, how it responded. Her nipples tightened and her pulse raced and she was right back to where she'd been last night, wanting to climb him like a tree in the kitchen and hold him down on the couch.

They needed to get out of this apartment. "We can try the museum." Because someplace loud and crowded and focused on a small child—she wouldn't be thinking about the way his eyes darkened when he looked at her or wondering if he looked as good without clothing as he did fully dressed.

No, no—she wasn't thinking about what his body looked like or how it'd felt under her hands or on top of her. Or in her. Or what might happen tonight after Marie went to bed.

She shifted in her chair. Nope. Not thinking about any of it.

"It's a date," Daniel said with a smile that bordered on wicked and Christine had to wonder how true that was.

Even when Daniel dressed down, he was sinfully gorgeous. Really, no one man should be able to make sweaters look that good—but Daniel did. Effortlessly.

What was ridiculous was that Daniel was crawling through a tunnel, chasing a squealing Marie and looking like he was having the time of his life. He wasn't normal, Christine realized. Normal men did not take an interest in other men's children. Normal men did not happily play with little girls. Normal men didn't...

Christine was off to the side, keeping an eye on the action in the tunnels from the ground. In that moment, she looked around and she saw something that surprised her.

There were a lot of men playing with a lot of children in this museum. Daniel by no means stuck out. What if Daniel *was* normal? Okay, overlooking the condo and the jet and the cars—what if he was a regular guy on the inside? What if...

Her father had never really played with her. She couldn't remember a single time she and her dad had done something fun together. Children were to be seen and not heard. Spare the rod and spoil the child.

She mentally flipped back through the few photo albums she'd studied before she'd left home for college. She'd known then that she'd never return because she couldn't live with her father's dictates for her behavior, her dress—the way she fixed her coffee, even. He had some ideal of what a daughter was and it'd been obvious that Christine wasn't it. She never would be.

She didn't remember a single photo of him holding her like Daniel had been holding Marie this morning. Not even when she was a baby. All the pictures were of her mother and Christine.

She wondered if Donna Murray would've liked Daniel. Her mother had been dead for almost ten years and in that time, Christine had learned to live with the loss. But now Christine couldn't help but wonder what her mom would've thought about all of this.

What if Daniel *was* normal and all the other men Christine had known weren't? What if Doyle was the aberration because he didn't want his own child? And her father—well, he was a megalomaniac.

Lost in thought, she watched Daniel carry Marie back to her as if they were walking out of a dream. What if this was a new normal?

Christine realized just from looking at her daughter that Marie was about ten minutes away from a total fun-based meltdown. Christine checked her phone—it was already eleven forty-five.

"Lunchtime—and then nap time." When Marie fussed at this announcement, Christine knew it was time to go.

Predictably, lunchtime was a disaster. Marie did not

want to leave the museum. She did not want to sit in a high chair. She did *not* want to be quiet. She didn't want Christine to hold her. She wanted Daniel, who had been upgraded from *"anal grr"* to *"my anal."*

Daniel did his best to help, but his mere presence only wound Marie up more and finally, Christine had to ask him to step back. She closed the door to Marie's room and sat in the glider with Marie in her arms, riding out the storm.

It took almost half an hour, but Marie finally cried herself out. Even better, Christine was able to get her into the portable crib without waking her up. She laid her daughter down and Marie rolled over, sound asleep.

Thank God. For a moment, Christine debated just curling up in the bed next to the crib and zoning out.

But then she thought of Daniel. At this very moment, he was somewhere in this condo, effortlessly making a sweater look hot. Would he be waiting on her, or would he merely be thankful that the screaming had stopped?

If she walked back into his living room, would he look at her like a woman or a problem?

She found him on the couch, toggling between a laptop and a cell phone. Crap, he was working. She started to back out, but he looked up.

"I didn't mean to bother you," she said quickly. "I'll let you get some work done."

He'd taken so much time off to fly her across the country and entertain her daughter. She didn't know how much longer this little time-out was going to last, but she couldn't expect him to put his entire life on hold because of her.

"Christine?" His voice stopped her and she turned back. He'd closed the computer and set it on the coffee table.

"I'll go. I should nap." It had been such a crazy couple of days and she was supposed to do an interview this evening. "I'll go," she said again, as if saying it would make it true.

It didn't. Because Daniel was already moving, his long legs effortlessly closing the distance between them. He looked at her with naked want.

"Stay," he said and then his hands were on her, sliding around her waist and pulling her into his chest. *"Stay."*

And fool that she was, she did. Last night, she'd taken what she'd wanted from him like a brazen hussy. Because that's who she was—who she'd always been. Desperate and needy and shamelessly chasing the high of a climax, no matter the cost. And Daniel had just…taken it. He'd taken everything she'd dished out—the anger, the lust, the need.

But today? Today, Daniel was in charge. She could feel it in the way his mouth moved over hers, the way his hands roved over her backside, pushing her closer to him. If she had half a brain, she'd stop this and go take that damned nap. Because she didn't need this and she didn't need him. All she needed was to know that her daughter was safe. Nothing else mattered.

"I want you," he growled against her neck—and then his teeth bit into her skin.

"Daniel," she moaned, digging her hands into his sweater and holding him close.

No. A moment of panic spiked through her. She couldn't do this. This wasn't who she was, not anymore. She was Christine Murray, loan processor and mom. Nothing more—and certainly not the kind of woman a man like Daniel went for.

She shoved him back, her chest heaving as if she'd run up all sixty-seven flights of stairs. "We can't do this." When he notched an eyebrow at her, heat rushed to her face and she added, "Again."

Daniel's hands slipped up her back and over her shoulders, stroking her lightly. "Why not?" he asked, his voice deceptively innocent. "We're two consenting adults. I enjoyed last night. I thought…" His hands stilled. "I thought you did, too."

"I did." He was easily the best lover she'd ever had. "But that doesn't change things."

"What things?" He cupped her cheeks in his hands again and stroked his thumbs over her skin.

She shouldn't lean into his touch, shouldn't want him. But she couldn't help it. "I don't know anything about you and I shouldn't trust you. And when this is all over, I'm going back to being a dumpy single mom and you'll go back to doing…whatever it is you do."

Everything about him sharpened. *Dangerous* was all she had time to think before he spoke. "You know more about me than anyone else does."

She stared at him—no way would she buy that line. But before she could tell him that, he went on, "And you do trust me. You trust me enough to get into a car and a plane with me. You trust me to play with your daughter. And," he said, which was when she realized he was backing her up, one slow step at a time, "you trust me with your body."

"I'm not worried about my body," she got out as they crossed the threshold into his bedroom.

He tilted his head to one side and leaned back, his hot gaze raking over her. "You're not? Then what's the problem?"

My heart, she wanted to tell him. She couldn't risk falling for him any more than she already had. Which was a battle she'd already lost because he was too perfect and she couldn't fight this attraction anymore.

His lips curved into a sinful smile. "Let me take care

of you, Christine," he said in a voice that made her want to do bad, bad things—like peel him out of that sweater.

Hell, she already wanted to do that. Last night on the couch had taken the edge off but she had a backlog of physical need that went well past a one-time thing.

"Why?" The younger Christine would've fallen right out of her pants by now—especially after what had happened last night.

But last night, she had been mad at him, at herself— at the world. The anger had tripped some sort of mental wire, sure. But today?

Today she was tired and worried. And Daniel was still...perfect.

"Why do you want me?"

Part of her hoped he would whisper sweet nothings, easy-to-believe lies about how pretty and special she was. But part of her knew that if he said things like that, she wouldn't believe him, no matter how sincere his earlier compliments had seemed. Having him think she was pretty wasn't enough for her to give her heart away again.

"Because you are the strongest woman I have ever met," he said in a serious voice that was a balm for her soul. "But even strong women need a soft place to land every now and then."

Oh, sweet heavens. She needed him and if that made her an unnatural thing, a sinner of the first order, then so be it.

And then he was kissing her, pulling her cardigan off and Christine gave in to the strength of his body and the sweetness of his lips. She gave in to this place out of time, this life that wasn't hers.

Daniel sat her down on the edge of the bed and pulled the tunic off over her head in one smooth movement. "Last night, you showed me what you wanted, Christine. So let me give it to you." When she shivered as the cold air rushed to her bare skin, he paused and said, "Okay?"

"Yeah. Kiss me." Because she didn't want to stop and think about this, or what would come after. She just wanted Daniel to take care of her.

With a wicked grin, he pushed her back on the bed. She yanked at the sweater, trying to get it over his head. Back in her wild youth, she would've let the guy take the lead. Whatever worked for him worked for her. She wasn't that girl anymore, thank God.

"I want you naked."

"The feeling is mutual." He pushed off her and peeled his sweater, shirt and undershirt off. So many layers. The joys of sex in the winter. But eventually, he was down to his bare chest. "Oh, my," Christine said, running her hands over his sculpted muscles. She jerked her gaze up to his face. "You really are perfect, aren't you?"

He chuckled, a throaty noise that was definitely strained with need. "Far from it." When she went for the button fly of his jeans, he grabbed her hands. "Patience," he hissed.

"I don't want to be patient." She didn't want time to think of all the reasons that doing this—again—was a bad idea. And she didn't want Marie to wake up before…

Well. Before Daniel unleashed another mind-blowing orgasm upon her body.

That's all this was, she tried to tell herself as she grabbed for his jeans again—something physical. A way to take the edge off.

This time, he was faster than she was. He dodged and grabbed her tank top, stripping it over her head.

And then she was in nothing but her bra and jeans. Daniel froze, staring down at her with what she desperately wanted to believe was reverence. "God, Christine—look at you." His hands drifted over her collarbones and to the tops of her breasts above her bra. "You are amazing."

She didn't want to think. "Less talk." This time, she got her hands on his jeans and began jerking the buttons open. Talking meant thinking and thinking wasn't what she wanted right now. She just wanted to feel *good*.

Daniel kicked out of his jeans but before he could get out of his boxer briefs, he had her on the bed, his mouth covering hers, his body covering hers. He was hot to the touch, so hot it made her sweat with need.

They rolled under the covers together. His hands were everywhere and his mouth followed in hot pursuit.

Christine's mind tried to drift off into the quicksand of worries and regrets—because she knew those things were real and unavoidable and would be waiting for her the moment the fun stopped.

But Daniel simply would not let her mind wander because he took full possession of her body. His erection rubbed against her in languid strokes, his mouth and hands demanding her full attention.

"All day," he murmured against the sensitive skin on the underside of her breasts, "I thought of doing this to you."

"You did?" Then she gasped when his fingers slid over her sex.

"I didn't get to touch you last night," he said, sounding cool when she was about to lose her mind. "At your request. But I want to touch you. All of you, Christine."

With that, he slid a finger inside of her. "Oh," she moaned, her hips writhing at his touch. Because he wasn't just stroking in and out of her body. Oh, no. He was kissing his way down to the juncture of her legs, rubbing his thumb over the very center of her sex—he was going to drive her insane.

"Daniel," she gasped as he worked over her body, his

mouth settling where his thumb had been. She laced her fingers into his short hair and held him against her.

Everything fell away as he drove her higher and higher. Good Lord, had anyone ever done this for her?

Daniel made a humming sound that rocketed through her and she couldn't help herself. Her back came off the bed and she made some kind of noise but her mind blanked out in white-hot pleasure and all she could think was how much she'd missed this.

How much she would miss this.

But before that thought could take hold and drag her to the future where she was alone, except for her daughter, Daniel moved over her. "That's better," he murmured, settling his weight on top of her. "God, you're so beautiful, Christine."

And she was so relaxed from the orgasm that she believed him. Because right now, she felt beautiful and desirable and special. He'd given that to her—all that and an orgasm, too. "You're very good at that."

He chuckled, a confident sound deep in his throat. Who knew chuckling could be so sensual? "I told you I'd take care of you," he said, pressing his erection against her opening. "And I always keep my promises." But instead of thrusting in, he paused. "Okay?"

She lifted her hips to meet him. "Please," she whimpered as he teased her.

"Hmm," he said, but this time, she heard the crack in his cool demeanor. "Which is better?" As he spoke, he flexed, driving his erection into her a teasing inch at a time. "When you're mad at me? Or when you're begging?"

She dug her nails into his back. "I'll show you mad…"

But that was all it took. He sank into her, filling her so completely that she almost came again. She must have really scratched him because, with a grunt, he grabbed her hands from around his waist and held her wrists against the bed. "Last night I was at your mercy," he said, driving into her with such ruthlessness that it was all she could do to meet him. "Now you're at mine and so help me, Christine, you will come again."

"Oh, God," she whispered as she gave herself up to him.

For all his perfection, they fit together. He was relentless, driving into her over and over. She came and then came again as he groaned and collapsed onto her and she knew—

She was forever ruined for anyone but this man. Which was a damn shame because time was not their friend.

Exhaustion clawing at her, she hugged him tight, not caring that he was crushing her with his weight. She didn't want to let him go.

"Christine," Daniel said, his voice shaky as he leaned up on his forearms and brushed a lock of hair from her face.

She'd never heard him so uneven before. She got her eyes open to find him staring down at her, a look so intense that she was almost afraid—because this was the man who stopped at nothing.

Just when she couldn't take another second of being in his sights, he kissed her. "We've got some time," he said, rolling to the side and tucking her in his arms. "Sleep."

She might have protested but honestly? She was completely wrung out and even the simple touch of his arm around her waist and his heartbeat against her ear from where she was resting on his chest—everything pulled her into the nap.

So she went. Willingly.

Twelve

Daniel was a mess. His mother was on the way—which was fine. That was a part of the plan.

Natalie had also landed—again, all part of the plan. But she was bringing her husband, CJ, with her.

Daniel's brother.

And the hell of it was, he wasn't sure why the idea of Natalie and CJ waltzing into his apartment had him on edge. After the explosive afternoon sex with Christine, Daniel would have thought he'd be achieving peak mellow right about now.

After all, he'd essentially taken the morning off. He'd played with Marie and made love to Christine and...

And for one too-brief morning, he'd gotten a glimpse of what a different life looked like, one where he was a normal man instead of the heir to the Lee Enterprises fortune and Hardwick Beaumont's bastard son.

He did not enjoy this level of personal confusion. This

was exactly why he didn't let people just walk into his house—or his life. The results were too messy.

Still, when he went to wake up Christine, he found himself staring at her. All of this upset—it was because of her. She made him feel things, want things, that he'd long ago decided he'd never have and, therefore, never want.

But here she was, anyway—in his house and in his bed. She was in his life now and he had no idea what to do next. Except wake her up. After all, he still had most of a fully functional plan to protect her and Marie, thwart Brian White and Clarence Murray and...

And then what? After the dust had settled—and he'd been doing this long enough to know that the dust would settle eventually—what came next? Where were plans A, B and C?

For the first time in his life, he wasn't sure what came next. "Christine," he said gently, leaning down to touch her hair. Her eyelids fluttered. "You need to get up and get dressed."

Her eyes scrunched shut. "Why?" she murmured groggily. "Wanna stay here."

God, he'd love that—her in his bed?

But the moment the thought crossed his mind, he heard his grandfather's voice in his head, telling him had to marry the "right" girl. "People will be here soon. Do you really want Natalie to interview you nude in my bed?"

That did the trick. She sat up, clutching the sheet to her chest. "Oh, Lord, no. How long?"

Daniel knew he needed to put some distance between them. But she looked so gorgeous, her hair mussed and her shoulders bare. He knelt, one knee on the bed, and kissed her.

"Twenty minutes," he murmured against her lips. A man could get a lot done in twenty minutes.

She shoved him back. "I've got to—oh, Lord!" She hopped out of bed, pulling the sheet with her. "I've got to…" she repeated, gathering up her clothes and dashing into his bathroom.

Just before she closed the door, she turned around, the sheet falling to reveal the creamy sweep of her breast. His blood quickened as he jerked his gaze up to her face.

She shot him a knowing little smile—and then shut the door.

"Wow," he exhaled, forcing his body to stand down. He had to get through some unexpected family socializing and media management before he could follow up on that smile.

"Where is my little Marie?" Minnie said, all but running into the apartment, bags of toys hanging from her arms as she ignored Daniel completely.

Marie looked up from her bowl of Cheerios and squealed. Christine came running—Daniel noticed that she came from the direction of the guest room, not from his bathroom. "Is everything—oh, Minnie," she said with a warm smile, "you're here."

"Christine," Minnie said, a warm smile on her face as she dropped her presents for Marie and scooped the little girl up. "You're looking better. Did you sleep well?"

Christine flushed and, for a second, Daniel wondered if she was about to give them away. Not that there was anything wrong with consenting adults enjoying some time together.

But that's not how his mom would look at it. A physical relationship between him and Christine would only be further proof that Daniel had found a ready-made family.

"Yes—the bed was wonderful," Christine said, slanting him a sideways look.

That answer was good enough for his mother. She and Marie were off, talking in a mixture of English, Korean and Baby that not even Daniel had a hope of understanding.

Daniel moved to Christine's side, but he was surprised to see a look of sadness on her face as she watched his mom and Marie. "Okay?"

"It's fine," she said too quickly. She caught him staring at her and gave him a weak smile. "It's just going to be hard when we leave all of this behind. I mean, for Marie. She's not used to being spoiled like this—that's all," she said, color washing over her pale cheeks.

"Christine—" he started, but stopped because she was right. It would be hard when this ended. But end it would.

The amount of work he was ignoring to take care of this was snowballing and if he didn't get a handle on things soon, he'd be buried in an avalanche.

Besides, it wasn't like he could keep Christine and Marie here. They had their own lives. He couldn't imagine Christine giving up her job because doing so would put her at the mercy of someone else and she wouldn't do that.

"It'll be fine," she said, watching Minnie and Marie. But her eyes revealed the lie of her words.

Once again, Daniel was seized with some sort of urge to do something—anything—to make it better. But what? It was no stretch to say that he was out to sea here. His entire involvement with Christine Murray should have been limited to protecting Marie from the press. That was what he knew how to do—a concrete plan with actionable steps that led to a desired—and predictable—outcome.

At no point did any of those steps include him and Christine naked. Or even partially naked, as they had been last night.

Or as they would be again tonight.

Jesus, what was wrong with him? The fact that he was thinking about tonight instead of the interview or the imminent arrival of his brother—this was a problem.

He could work around problems. Through them, if he had to. And his attraction to Christine... Well, he didn't want to call it a problem. Even if it was on the verge of becoming one.

His phone buzzed—the text from the doorman. Natalie and CJ were here. Which was good. It would keep Daniel from thinking about Christine and her sleepy smiles and the way she had felt beneath him, over him. "They're on their way up."

Christine patted her hair. "Do I look all right?"

"Gorgeous. As usual." Even as the words were leaving his mouth he wondered where they had come from. He did not flirt. He didn't even sweet talk. He was all business.

Except with her. And he didn't know why.

Luckily, he was saved from any further fruitless introspection by a knock on the door. He opened it to see CJ wearing a giant cowboy hat. "You really do live here," his half brother said, an easy smile on his face. But that's how CJ was. He was open and happy, honest almost to a fault.

"I really do live here." It struck Daniel that, if not for Christine, he had no idea when he might've invited his brother to Chicago. "Come on in. Thanks for making the trip, you two."

"And miss the chance to get a glimpse into the life of Daniel Lee?" Natalie said, launching a professional smile in his direction. "We wouldn't miss *this* for the world."

Daniel knew that she was teasing him—they both were. But it bothered him, anyway. He didn't really have close friends. He suddenly had a huge family—but they were mostly strangers. It had always been easier that way. Safer, too. "It's not that big of a deal, guys."

It was supposed to be a joke. But he didn't miss the look that Natalie and CJ shared, the way they seemed to understand each other without saying a word.

He shook his head. He shouldn't have stayed in bed with Christine until she'd fallen asleep. It had messed with his normal routine and that was throwing him for a loop. "My mother is here. She's going to watch Marie during the interview," he told them as he led them into the front room.

CJ whistled at the view, which got Christine's attention. She hopped to her feet and said, "Hello. I'm Christine Murray," in a surprisingly even voice, given the circumstances.

"CJ Wesley," CJ said, giving her a big handshake and another easy smile. "It's a pleasure to make your acquaintance. This is my wife, Natalie."

Daniel watched Christine closely as she and Natalie made their introductions. He could tell Christine was nervous but she was doing an admirable job of hiding it. That was encouraging.

Minnie came over with Marie. Daniel introduced his mother and Christine introduced her daughter and Marie introduced Daniel to everyone as *"my anal!"* which sent CJ into snorting peals of laughter. It should have been awful. All of these people were in Daniel's condo where, prior to this, only his mother and the maid had ever set foot.

He didn't know what to do. For all of his training on manners, Grandfather had never prepared Daniel for this—his brother was talking to his mother and Natalie talking to Christine and Marie being passed around and smiling big for everyone. It wasn't bad. He watched all the pieces of his life collide head-on and it was...

Okay. This was okay. He could have his half brother and his mother and his—well, he wasn't sure what Christine was. But he could have all of them here together and somehow, it worked.

Christine looked up at him, her eyes wide. She quirked an eyebrow and he could almost hear her saying, *are you all right?* And he realized he was standing off to the side, watching them, without being a part of the conversation.

Natalie noticed Christine's distraction and turned to face him. "We should get started. Where do you want us?"

Yes, it would probably be best to cut the chitchat short and focus on the reason they were all here today. This wasn't a party, after all.

"This way." He led them back to his office.

While Christine had slept, he had arranged some lights and chairs. "Do you need me for anything?"

Natalie smiled at the setup. "We'll go over the talking points and then take a run at it. But," she added, looking up, "I want a tour when we're done. We came all this way—don't think you're going to get us out of here without at least showing us around."

He scowled at her. "You know you're more than welcome to—"

She made shooing gestures, which made Christine giggle. "I've got this. Go have a beer with CJ."

Right. That was probably what normal people did—grabbed a beer with their brother. Except Daniel had never done that. Not outside of the Beaumont Brewery and tastings with Zeb, that was.

Feeling awkward in his own home, Daniel found his brother standing by the window, looking down on Navy Pier.

"Damn, if I had any idea that you had a place like this, I would've invited myself a long time ago," he said in a quiet voice when Daniel approached with two Beaumont beers in hand. CJ took one and said, "You don't mind that I came, do you?"

"Of course not. You're family."

They stood for a moment, the silence uncomfortable. Or maybe it wasn't. Daniel didn't like the way he was suddenly unsure. Uncertainty was a liability and liabilities were dangerous.

CJ leaned to one side and looked over Daniel's shoulder to where Minnie and Marie were singing. "Your mom seems like a nice person."

"She is."

For some reason, that statement made CJ smile. "I wonder about you sometimes, man."

Daniel took a long pull of his beer, trying to figure out which way this conversation was going. "How so?"

CJ still had that easygoing smile, but there was a hardness to his eyes that Daniel recognized. As much as he didn't want to admit it, CJ was a Beaumont, just like Daniel. "You do realize that I've never even been to your place in Denver? If it hadn't been for Christine, how long would it have been before I saw this fabulous view?"

Daniel tried to shrug nonchalantly. "You're welcome anytime. You know that."

"Do I?" CJ chuckled, but it wasn't a happy sound. "I guess I'm not surprised," he said, turning his attention back to the view.

"About what?"

"This," CJ said, gesturing to the world below. "This is just how you are, isn't it? You keep yourself removed from the rest of us—even those who care for you. You're always distant and remote and watching."

He'd argue that—but he couldn't because it was true. Hadn't he just stood on the perimeter of his own living room and watched everyone else talk—without him? Instead, Daniel heard himself ask, "Does it bother you?"

"What?" CJ asked, taking another pull of his beer.

"Well, your mom's Mexican American but your dad—both of your dads," he hurried to add, "are American. Does it ever bother you, trying to be both?"

CJ gave him a look of utter confusion. "No," he said slowly. "It's never been an either/or thing."

Of course it wasn't for CJ and Daniel felt stupid for having asked. But who else besides Zeb and CJ would ever understand?

Except even they couldn't, of course. It was one thing to be one of Beaumont's biracial bastards—but there was no way to compare Zeb being half black or CJ being half Mexican with Daniel being half Korean. Minnie was a citizen now—but she hadn't been when Daniel had been born.

CJ took another drink. "I will say this, though—I'm still working on how to be a Wesley and a Beaumont. There's been a hard line between those two things my entire life and it's only since I've known Natalie that I've been able to think about crossing the streams. It's a difficult thing, trying to carve out a place to exist where people said you couldn't." He was silent for a moment longer and then slid a sideways glance to Daniel. "Why?"

"No reason." Unexpectedly, Daniel was glad CJ had come. His brother might not ever understand what it was like to be Lee Dae-Won's grandson, but he knew what it was like to be Hardwick Beaumont's bastard.

Because hadn't that been at the center of Daniel's entire relationship with his grandfather? He'd stained the honor of the Lee family name by being born. It was his duty to restore that honor—or else.

Marie squealed behind them and both men turned to

look. "She seems nice—Christine, not the baby. Although the baby seems nice, too. As far as babies go, anyway."

"Don't read anything into it." It was bad enough that Daniel's mother was already seeing grandbabies. He didn't need CJ joining in. "This was simply the best way to make sure she was protected until the dust settled."

CJ gave him another long look and Daniel knew he wasn't buying that line. "Whatever, man. You don't have to justify your actions to me." For a moment, Daniel thought CJ wouldn't let it go. Then he sighed deeply. "Again, I'm sorry for crashing. Natalie's settling into ranch life but... I think she needed a break and I sure as hell wasn't going to pass up the chance to see Chicago." He smacked Daniel on the shoulder. "Thanks for getting us that room at the Drake."

"No problem," Daniel said, more relieved than he expected to be at the subject change. "My driver will take you wherever you guys want to go after Natalie and Christine are done."

"But until then," CJ said, with a gleam in his eyes that Daniel didn't necessarily like, "I'm going to hang out with your mom and see what I can learn about the mysterious Daniel Lee."

Daniel groaned. But even as he cringed at the thought of his mother sharing baby stories with CJ, he felt a little excited about it, too. He wasn't any good at having brothers—but even though the situation made him uncomfortable, there was something reassuring about the way things had played out.

Natalie and Christine were talking. CJ started rolling a ball to Marie, all while talking and joking with Minnie. And Daniel?

He was glad they were here. But more than that, he didn't want to stand on the edge, watching from a distance.

What if CJ were right? What if it were possible to carve out a new space—a place where he could be both Daniel and Dae-Hyun? A place where he could honor his father and his grandfather and still be his own man?

Daniel looked toward his office, where Natalie and Christine were conducting their interview. He had dragged Christine through the mud two years ago. And yet she'd put her trust in him—that he could shield her and Marie, that he could take care of her. She made him want things he hadn't thought he could want.

In her eyes, Daniel was almost…forgiven.

Christine waited awkwardly while Natalie set up tripods with phones and tablets attached to them. She would record from several different angles so they had options when Natalie spliced the video. Christine thought. She hadn't understood all the technical terms.

"So tell me," Natalie said, adjusting one of the devices. "How did you wind up here with Daniel?" When Christine didn't answer immediately, Natalie went on, "I'm not recording. I'm just curious. I've been working with him for months now and he's like Fort Knox. We can't get him out to the ranch. CJ wasn't even invited today but he couldn't pass up the opportunity to find out a little bit more about his half brother."

"Honestly? I have no idea. One moment, there were reporters barking at the bank and I was afraid. The next thing I know, Daniel's whisked me away on his private jet and I'm meeting his mother in this condo." Natalie notched an eyebrow at her and Christine realized that might have sounded whiny. "It's great—don't get me wrong. But it all happened so fast."

Too fast, it seemed. If she stopped and thought about it—like she was doing right now—everything was a blur.

Except for the part where Daniel took her to bed. And made her climax three times before letting her nap. *That* she remembered perfectly.

She desperately hoped that whatever was happening between her and Daniel wasn't just really good sex. The kind of sex she wasn't sure she'd ever had before.

The kind of sex she was not going to regret. Sleeping with Daniel was the same as wearing these expensive clothes or jetting around the country in his private plane. This wasn't real life and it wouldn't last.

She started to tell herself that she still didn't trust him—but she knew that wasn't true. He was right—she trusted him with her life, with her daughter's life. She trusted him with her body.

But she didn't know him. Even if what he had said was true, that she knew more about him than almost anyone else in the world—she still didn't know who Daniel Lee was.

And she had to accept the fact that she wasn't going to find out. She didn't need to find out, either. She just needed to…get back to normal.

Back to her job at the bank while Marie was in day care. Back to the long nights and the housework that piled up. Back to the crushing loneliness.

Boy, she was really selling it.

"I hope you don't mind me saying so, but that's just… Well, that's not like Daniel. I assume. He's family, but we know so little about him." Natalie adjusted one of the monitors and asked, "Can you sit back just a few inches— perfect." She sat in the chair opposite of Christine. "I tried to look him up, you know. Before I went digging for CJ."

"You did?" Because Christine had also tried looking Daniel up and hadn't been able to find anything. She'd assumed that was because she hadn't been looking in the right places. "What did you find?"

Natalie leaned back in her chair, looking defeated. "Nothing. Not a damn thing. And it's not because he never did anything newsworthy. It was like there was a Daniel Lee–shaped black hole where nothing existed. He's still like that. I mean, I had no idea what his mother's name was. And he stood up with CJ at our wedding!" she said, her frustration bleeding through.

Christine could sympathize. "I didn't know I was going to meet her until she opened the door. I think she was almost as surprised as I was, frankly." She debated whether or not she should tell Natalie what she had learned—but then again, what *had* she learned? Not much. "He told you what happened two years ago, didn't he?"

Natalie nodded. "But that's the other thing," she said, reaching over and adjusting a light. "I honestly think he feels bad about what he did to you—and trust me, he is not the kind of guy to experience guilt. Before you came along, if someone had told me that underneath that handsome face, he was actually a robot, I wouldn't have been surprised."

Christine felt her cheeks heat as she dropped her gaze to her lap. "He's apologized for dragging my name through the mud. I guess all of *this*," she said, waving her hands over her clothes and around the room and toward Natalie, "is his way of making up for it."

Natalie didn't say anything and Christine glanced up to find the other woman staring at her. "Well," she said slowly, "I'm glad to hear it. Are you ready to get started?"

Not really. She understood why she needed to do this interview, but that didn't make it any better. She was so loath to have her name out there in any capacity that it was almost physically painful to say, "We might as well get this over with."

"Okay," Natalie said as she reached over and tapped the

screens. Then, in what Christine recognized as Natalie's television voice, she said, "Ms. Murray, how would you describe your relationship with your father?"

Thirteen

Christine woke with a start, her heart pounding. Fragments of a dream where she was being interviewed not by Natalie but by her father—"Tell me about your relationship with me," he asked—floated through her mind. It took a moment to remember where she was.

She was in Daniel's bed. After his family had left and Marie had gone to sleep, he had carried her back to his bed and made love to her again. She'd felt safe and happy and beautiful.

She flung out her arm at the same time a noise hit her ears. The bed was empty.

Now fully awake, she got up and fumbled with her nightgown. As she dressed, she strained to hear the familiar sounds of Marie's cries and checked the clock.

2:00 a.m. Right on schedule.

Except the sound she heard wasn't Marie. She tiptoed out into the hall and saw a dim glow in the living room. She saw Daniel sitting on the couch, bathed in the blue light of computer screens. He was speaking Korean and sounding angry.

Quietly, Christine went to check on Marie. But for once, the little girl was sound asleep in the middle of the night. Christine felt awful for being awake when her daughter was out like a light, but...

She slipped back into the living room. Daniel turned and, without missing a beat in whatever he was saying, held out his hand for her.

She took it and sank against his side of the couch. He had a headset on, so she couldn't hear the other half of the conversation—not that she would've understood it, anyway. Daniel's laptop was open and he was toggling between several screens—all of which were filled with numbers and Korean writing she had no hope of understanding.

But he tucked his arm around her shoulders and she nestled in, letting the flow of his words lull her into a daze. It was silly to think that this felt right. The last time she'd thought things felt right between her and a man, it had been with Doyle and see where that had gone? And besides, this wasn't her life. In a few short days, things would go back to normal and she would be okay. Really.

"Sorry about that," Daniel said some time later as he pulled his headset off and closed the laptop. "I didn't mean to wake you, but it was a meeting I couldn't miss."

"It's all right." They sat for a moment longer before she asked, "Would you tell me something about yourself?"

She expected him to tense up and pull away. But he didn't. "Like what?"

She snuggled in deeper. He was *so* warm. "Anything. No one knows anything about you. Natalie said she didn't even know your mother's name before today."

He sighed and she wondered if he would avoid this

topic—again. Then he opened the laptop. After several clicks, she found herself looking at a website. It was in Korean, but there were pictures. An older man scowled out at them, looking harsh and unforgiving—and vaguely like Daniel. With a few keystrokes, the page was translated into English.

"This is my grandfather," he said in a soft voice. "Lee Dae-Won. He was the founder of Lee Enterprises, and he helped industrialize Korea after the Korean War."

Christine stared at the man. "He doesn't look very happy."

"In Korea, it's not common to smile for pictures." He chuckled. "But you're right. He wasn't the jolliest of men. I spent every summer with him, whether I wanted to or not. I was his only grandchild."

They sat in silence while Christine skimmed the text. Lee Enterprises had been founded in 1973 by Lee Dae-Won. It started with one factory making parts for transistor radios and from there had spawned an empire—factories, real estate—a little bit of everything. "Wow," she said when she read that the company was valued at $200 billion. The number was almost too big to be real. "So your grandfather was one of the richest men in Korea?"

"Pretty much. And as much as he hated it, I was his only heir."

There was something in his voice that made her pause. "Why did he hate it?"

"Because I was his great shame," Daniel said, leaning his head back. "Not only was I born out of wedlock, but my father was American. For three months every year, my grandfather did his best to make me into the perfect heir. He wanted me to marry a good Korean girl—from a family of his choosing—so the line would continue. That was the only way he thought I could redeem my bad birth." He sat up and smirked at her, as if what he'd just said wasn't that important, when Christine had the feeling that it was everything. "In the end, I won. I refused to marry and when he died, I took control of the company."

This, Christine realized, was the Daniel Lee–shaped black hole Natalie had been referring to. "No one knows this about you?"

"No." He turned his attention back to the laptop. With a few more keystrokes, he pulled up a different page. "Because, in Korea, my name is Lee Dae-Hyun. He didn't allow me to be Daniel when I was with him." Christine stared at the website. There was his name, listed on the board of directors. But there was no picture and no biography.

"I thought…" she said slowly, trying to wrap her head around it. "I thought you were a political consultant."

"I am. I mean, I was. My grandfather taught me a lot about manipulating the press and controlling appearances. By the time I went to college, I'd learned how to cover my tracks. I didn't want him watching me and I didn't want people to find out how much I was worth. If men like Brian White—" Christine physically shuddered at the mention of the name. "Yeah, that. If he knew that I was a billionaire…"

"Wait." Christine sat up. "You're a *billionaire*?"

His smile tightened. "It changes things, I know."

She didn't know why she was surprised. After all, it made sense. He owned three homes in two different countries. He had a private jet on standby at all times. Everything in this apartment—he really *was* rich. She just hadn't put a dollar amount to that. "Does it, though?"

It was physically painful, the way his self-deprecating smile faded into something that looked much sadder. "It does." He cupped her cheek in his hand. "You're the first woman I've ever brought home with me. I don't know what it is about you, Christine. Two years ago, I knew that I was crossing a line. But it was too late—I couldn't stop what I'd started." He stroked his thumb over her cheek. "I don't regret making sure your father lost. But after what I did to you, I realized—that was what my grandfather would have done. He would've looked for weaknesses and exploited them mercilessly. It didn't matter how innocent anyone was, not to him. And I..." his voice trailed off.

"And you're not him," she said, her voice gentle.

She could tell by the way he grimaced that he didn't quite believe that. "After the election, I got out of the game. Zeb had decided to get control of the brewery and I knew I could help him accomplish his goals." He touched his forehead to hers. "I spent so long trying not to be the man my grandfather demanded but when it came down to the important things—to someone like you—I realized I was exactly the man he'd created. And I couldn't be that person anymore."

She tucked her head back against his chest and tried to make sense of it all. Even if it were the middle of the afternoon and she was fully awake, she wasn't sure she could.

As she thought back through everything he had just said—all those secrets he carried—one thing stuck out. She pushed herself off his chest and looked him in the eyes. "He was wrong about you," she told him, hearing echoes of something he had said to her just a few days ago.

His gaze shuttered. "What?"

"All those things he said—because he said them to you, right? That you weren't Korean enough, that you weren't *good* enough? He was wrong. Just as my father is wrong about me."

He looked away. "I know that. I've known that for years."

"But it's one thing to *know* it and another thing to *believe* it," she pressed. "I don't know what it's like to have an unforgiving grandfather or what it's like to be a part of two cultures or two families who don't know what to do with you. But I do know what it's like to grow up with a man who believes your very existence was a mistake and I know what it's like to have that voice in your head reminding you how wrong you are no matter what you do or how hard you try."

That had been her whole life, hadn't it? Trying to meet some impossible standard that would always be out of reach because, according to her father, she was a daughter of Eve and therefore a sinner. And she'd long ago decided that if she would always be a sinner, she might as well earn that title.

"You don't have to be the person he says you are or should be. And..." Unexpectedly, her eyes started to water. "And you don't have to prove anything to him. My father will never know me and he'll never know his granddaughter because that's his choice. Who am I to argue with him?"

She'd thought she had made peace with this years ago. But she had proven herself wrong. The first time she'd had sex with Daniel—hadn't she decided that if wanting him made her an unnatural sinner of the first order, so be it? Those weren't her words—they were her father's. Even when she'd thought she had built a wall between them, he *still* found his way into her head.

Daniel looked at her with such tenderness that she didn't know what to make of it. "How can you stand it?" he asked. "How can you sit there and treat me like I'm a decent human being, after what I did to you?"

She'd spent the better part of the last few weeks asking herself the same question. And she wasn't any closer to an answer. "I don't know. But we were both different people then, weren't we? I changed because of what happened two years ago. And I think…" she touched his face. "I think you did, too."

"I don't know. I don't think I changed enough." He tried to look away, back to the computer screen and the other half of his life that no one else knew about.

But she wouldn't let him. "Why did you tell me about this?" she asked, waving at the screen.

He shrugged as if he were trying to look nonchalant and failing miserably. "You're here. I owe you an explanation for why I was calling into a board meeting at two in the morning."

"I don't believe that for one second, Daniel Lee. It's because you trust me." She took a deep breath, knowing it was the truth. "Just like I trust you. I forgive you for what happened two years ago, Daniel. I forgive you," she repeated and the words seemed to lift a weight off her shoulders.

Something flitted across his face that she couldn't interpret. "I can't promise you anything, Christine. We've got another day or two but beyond that…"

Beyond that, there couldn't be anything between them. Their worlds were too different. "I don't want any promises, Daniel." Because if he didn't make any promises, then, when they went their separate ways, she wouldn't be disappointed if he didn't keep them. "Let's just enjoy what we've got for the time being."

He stared at her for the longest moment. "Come on," he said, pulling her to her feet. "It's time to go to bed."

Like all good things, Daniel's time with Christine came to an end. And when it did, he wished that it hadn't.

For two more days, they essentially played house.

Christine slept in his bed. They ate their meals around the table and visited the Chicago Children's Museum at the Pier a second time. Minnie came over to play with Marie.

Daniel got the chance to do something he rarely did— he relaxed and had fun. True, he couldn't ignore reality for long. He had to get up for another middle of the night call to the board of Lee Enterprises. And he constantly monitored the impact of Christine's interview. But when all that was done, she was waiting for him in bed.

Something had changed between them. He didn't want to be so naïve as to think those three little words—"I forgive you"—were the reason why. They were just words and, besides, he didn't exactly deserve her forgiveness.

He didn't deserve her at all—not her affection, not her trust. He didn't deserve Marie's sweet smiles or her silly nickname for him. Christine was convinced she wasn't good enough for him because of her past and his wealth— but she had it all wrong.

He wasn't good enough for her. Because if he were, he'd be able to keep his hands off her. He'd be able to give her space.

And he couldn't, selfish bastard that he was.

As a piece of marketing, the interview was a success. It got some good press and one cable news show spent an hour debating whether or not Christine really had an impact on any election, present or past. Natalie fielded the media requests, but—aside from one or two news outlets that were clearly looking to sell a particular angle—the interview diffused the gossip.

It also helped that Clarence Murray got a challenger in the Republican field—a state senator who just happened to be a moderate while at the same time being a Methodist minister. He was conservative but not on the fringe.

Daniel could see Brian White's hand at work as the Murray campaign pivoted, leaving Christine behind.

Which meant their time was almost up. Daniel needed to get her back to her life. But more than that, he needed to get back to his own—board meetings and beer tastings and expensive condominiums around the world, always watching. Back to being alone and somehow thinking that kept his grandfather from dictating his choices in life.

No, that wasn't true. He had things to do—companies to run, situations to monitor. He had plenty to keep him busy. Except…

If Daniel chose to be alone in order to spite the old man—who'd been dead for almost thirteen years—then wasn't he still letting his grandfather dictate his choices?

It didn't matter. What mattered was that he made his peace with Christine and fulfilled his promise to protect her and Marie. He was a man of honor. Maybe his grandfather would've been proud of him for that, if nothing else.

Christine refused to take any of the clothes and toiletries, so Daniel left instructions to have everything boxed up and mailed to her. It wasn't like he had any use for ladies' tops or toddler jammies.

His mother came over to say goodbye and Daniel was stunned when Minnie got teary. "You take care," she told Christine, sniffing, patting Christine's cheek and rubbing Marie's back. "And if there's anything I can ever do for you, please let me know."

"I will," Christine said, wrapping an arm around his mother and hugging her tight.

This tearful farewell made him feel things he didn't think he was capable of feeling.

Emotion was a weakness, a vulnerability. If he cared about something, that something—or someone—could be used against him. At one point, he had loved his grandfather. He had wanted his grandfather's approval and the old man had used that against him, always dangling a kind word or an affectionate pat on the shoulder just out of Daniel's reach, like a carrot tied to the end of the long stick.

That hadn't changed. If Brian White ever figured out that Daniel cared for Christine and Marie, Daniel knew what would happen. The man would come after them with guns drawn and murder in his eyes. White would convince himself his actions were justified because Daniel had dared care about someone.

Because he did. It was pointless to deny it. He cared for Christine. He cared for Marie.

So the best way to keep them safe was to stay away from them. He would go back to doing what he should have done from the very beginning—monitoring the situation from a distance, running interference with an invisible hand. He would keep Natalie involved for as long as needed. He would be vigilant. There was no room for error.

So why did this feel like such a mistake?

The flight back to Denver was nearly silent. What was there to say? He had already screwed up her life enough. Doing anything foolish like asking to see her again or even asking her to come home with him—even for one more night—would only prolong the inevitable.

Daniel had, of course, planned for every contingency upon their arrival back in Denver. When the jet doors opened, suddenly he found himself talking. "Porter Cole is here with your car. I've arranged for him or one of his associates to shadow you for the next week or two, just to be safe." Her eyebrows jumped up. "But I don't think you'll have any problems. The news cycle has moved on. You should be fine from here on out."

She was silent as they gathered up Marie and walked

down the jet's stairs. "So," Christine said as they headed to her car. "This is it?"

What he should've said was *yes*. A clean break. No one would ever draw a connection between Christine Murray and Daniel Lee. It was better this way.

But that's not what came out of his mouth. "For now. You still have my number?" She nodded. "Call me anytime, if there's anything you need. Anytime," he repeated, pointedly *not* cupping her cheek in his hand and *not* pulling her into an embrace.

Marie blinked up at him sleepily. *"My anal,"* she murmured around the thumb in her mouth.

"My Marie," he said, patting her back. "You be good for Mommy, okay?"

Christine buckled her daughter into the car seat and then turned back to Daniel, her face so blank it hurt to see it. "You won't call me, will you?"

Daniel had never let himself fall in love and, therefore, had never let his heart get broken. He wondered if this was what it felt like. "No."

She tried to smile, but the corner of her mouth pulled down into a frown. "I see." Then, unexpectedly, she threw her arms around his neck and kissed him and, fool that he was, he let her. He did more than that. He held her tight and kissed her back, thinking that this was it. *The End*.

"Phones work both ways," she whispered. With that, she climbed into her car. With a dawning sense of horror, all Daniel could do was watch her drive away.

"That must have been some trip to Chicago," Porter said as he walked over to Daniel. "You're really going to let her go?"

"Aren't you supposed to be following her?" he demanded, trying his best to ignore the stab of... something Porter's observation sparked in his chest.

"Yes, sir," Porter said with a mocking salute. He climbed into his own vehicle and took off, leaving Daniel alone.

Just like always.

He could call her. Just to check in, see how she was doing. He could ask about Marie, make sure she got the clothes and things. He could…

No. To keep in contact with Christine—or, worse, see her—would be a risk. To both of them.

So what if he'd been able to relax around her? So what if he'd brought her to his home, his bed? So what if he'd told her who he really was and so the hell *what* that she had understood, damn it—understood the impossible burdens his grandfather had put upon Daniel's shoulders at an age when most kids were worried about learning to ride bikes and play video games?

None of it mattered, as long as she was safe from the damage he'd unleashed upon her life. From him.

She might have forgiven him.

But he couldn't forgive himself.

Fourteen

A week passed. Christine tried to go back to normal. She returned to her job at the bank and made up a story about staying with an old college friend. Not that Sue or anyone else at the bank bought that, but they didn't press her.

Things with Marie were rough. The little girl wanted to do all of the fun things with Daniel and Minnie. And when neither of those two people appeared, she threw a fit that seemed to last for days.

Which just reminded Christine how much she had enjoyed the vacation, as well. It'd been such a relief to have Minnie there to watch Marie for a little bit while she...

It felt wrong to admit that it had been a relief not to have to think about Marie—but it was the truth. For a few days, she had taken some time for herself.

And what had she done with that time?

Nothing much. She'd only fallen in love with Daniel.

She wanted to think that, with time and space, she

would get over it. The daily grind would wear her down until that time in Chicago was little more than a dream.

It had very nearly been a dream come true.

More than once, Christine called up Daniel's contact information. She hadn't heard from him. She hadn't expected to—but there'd been a kernel of hope that he'd miss her, that maybe she'd meant something to him.

After all, he'd told her about his life in Korea and his grandfather and the fact that Daniel was a billionaire but worked as an executive vice-president in a midsized brewery in Denver, of all things. He trusted her. He liked her. He'd introduced her to his mother, for crying out loud.

These thoughts were the quickest way to madness because he had also told her he would always keep his word and he had, for better or for worse, promised that he would not call her again. And he hadn't.

She knew he wouldn't. The simple fact was that, until he accepted that she'd forgiven him for what had happened two years ago, he wouldn't.

No, that wasn't right. She wouldn't hear from him until he'd forgiven himself. And she didn't know if he was capable of doing that.

Which was reassuring, in an odd sort of way. He wasn't treating her like a convenient bed buddy. Which was why she wasn't going to call him, either. She simply didn't want him to think she was only interested in him because of what he could do for her—the clothes, the jet, the luxury condo.

All of those things were nice but they weren't what made Daniel who he was.

He was gorgeous and rich, true. And maybe for a lot of people, that would've been enough. But he was also the only man who had ever stood up for her, with her. Every other man had cut her loose the moment the shit hit the fan. Her father had turned on her and Doyle had abandoned her. But Daniel?

He ran toward the danger. He told her she was worth defending.

More than that, he made her feel beautiful and whole and valuable—things she had been taught she didn't deserve.

Then the boxes arrived—four boxes of designer clothes and makeup, toys and outfits for Marie. There was no note—of course there wasn't. But they were from him.

She sat in her bedroom, staring at it all and trying not to cry. The cardigan she'd worn the afternoon he'd taken her to bed was in there—she lifted it out and it smelled like him.

This was fine. Everything was okay. All these things were just…souvenirs from the most unusual, wonderful vacation she'd ever had. Yes, that was it. And she was only sad because the vacation was over. Not because she didn't know if Daniel had sent her these boxes to purge any trace of her from his apartment—and his life—or if he'd wanted to make sure she had something to remember him by.

Because she certainly wasn't ever going to forget him.

It was Sunday—two and a half weeks since Christine had returned to Denver a changed woman. Marie was having a fussy morning after a night of broken sleep but Christine was going to church, darn it. Because if she sat home with Marie, she would start to wallow in unproductive self-pity and who had time for that? Not her. Besides, Marie was already wallowing enough for both of them.

Marie cried all the way to the church and Christine felt like crying, too. She just needed to get her bearings again, she decided. Work had been blissfully quiet and political consultants had left her alone. But it was perfectly reasonable to say that the events of the previous month had left her shaken. She and Marie just had to get back to normal, that was all.

Which was all well and good—but try telling a fourteen-month-old that.

By the time they made it to the Red Rock church, Marie had almost cried herself out. Christine carried her inside, already mentally apologizing to the day care ladies and hoping that Marie would keep it together long enough that Christine could find some comfort in the service.

"I want my Daniel," Marie whimpered pitifully, although it came out sounding like *"Wan anal."*

"I know, sweetie. But you'll have fun today," Christine promised in a voice that was obnoxiously perky even to her own ears.

Normally, Christine could lose herself in the service. She enjoyed the chance to reconnect with her faith and the music wasn't bad either. But today, all she could think about was how she would cushion her little girl's disappointment that "her Daniel" wasn't here and then, when Marie finally went to bed, how Christine would deal with her own disappointment that Daniel wasn't going to call.

No. Better not think of it.

After the service, she went down to get Marie from the day care. Marie fussed some more as they followed the crowd out of the building. Then, suddenly, she squirmed in Christine's arms and squealed in what sounded like... excitement?

"Hey!" Christine said, struggling to hold on to her daughter. But Marie somehow wiggled out of her coat and slid to the floor with an unceremonious *plop.* Then she was off, walking on wobbly legs through the crowded lobby.

"Marie!" Christine cried, struggling to get through the crowd before her daughter got trampled. She lost sight of

Marie for just a second and then, when the crowd parted, Marie wasn't there.

Panic dumped into Christine's bloodstream as she frantically looked around—who had her daughter? Marie wasn't fast enough to just *disappear*.

Then she came to a screeching halt because someone did have Marie. Someone tall and dark, someone who made cable-knit sweaters look surprisingly glamorous.

Oh, God—*Daniel*.

She'd never been so glad to see anyone in her entire life. "You're here," she said in shock.

"I am," he agreed, giving Marie a hug. The little girl threw her arms round his neck, screaming with delight.

Christine's heart melted at the sight of them together. "What are you doing here?"

He smiled hesitantly. "Is there someplace we can go to talk?" he asked, his eyes intent as the rest of the church slowly emptied out around them. "Someplace inconspicuous?"

He had come for her. Not under the cover of darkness, not just for sex. At least, she hoped. That kernel of hope took root in her chest and began to blossom into something far greater. "Come with me."

They went back down to the place where it all started— the old living room set outside the day care. Back to the place where it had first occurred to her that maybe he'd come to help after all.

As they walked down the stairs, though, a horrible thought occurred to her. What if he wasn't here for her? What if something else had happened and she was back in the news again? What if he were only here because of his misguided sense of protecting her?

What if he didn't feel about her the way she felt about him?

Paralyzed by this thought, she sat awkwardly in the

exact spot she had sat so many weeks ago. "Has some-thing gone wrong?"

He cuddled Marie, then put her down. She went off to get a book, chattering happily about "her Daniel." "No," he said, standing in front of her. "Nothing's happened."

"Okay…" How she was supposed to take that?

"I mean—something did happen." He looked anxious again, which didn't help her nerves. "But it doesn't con-cern your father's political campaign or your reputation on the internet."

"That's…good?"

She hadn't seen him this unsettled since he'd told her about his grandfather and his business in Korea.

"I miss you," he blurted out. "I didn't expect to. I've never missed anyone before. But I miss you."

He said it like it'd come as a complete and total surprise to him. And frankly, she was a little surprised herself. "I miss you, too," she said, pushing herself out of the chair. She didn't want him looking down on her. She wanted to meet him as an equal. "But you made it clear that there wasn't anything else to our relationship. You've atoned for your mistakes in the past and I've forgiven you. Every-thing else was just an…unexpected bonus."

Somehow, he managed to look ashamed by this state-ment. "That's how it was supposed to be. But that's not how it worked out. I…" He took a deep breath and took her hands in his. "I thought I could go back to the way I was before. I thought I would be fine without you—with-out anyone. Watching and waiting—always *above* every-one else. Never *with* them. Does that even make sense?"

She thought back to his apartment, looking down on the world but never touching it—or anyone in it. "I think so. You never had anyone come over to your place before and then suddenly Marie and I were there and your brother and Natalie…"

He stepped in closer, close enough that she could feel the warmth of his chest through her layers. "I thought I could go back to watching you from a distance—monitoring you online, having Porter shadow you. But I missed you, Christine." He sounded continually surprised by this realization.

She smiled in spite of herself. "You said that already."

He took a deep breath and for some reason, she thought of a man standing on a bridge, ready to jump. "I thought about what you said to me that one night on the couch. I don't have to prove anything to my grandfather. I never did. But I thought that, by keeping my distance from my family and never getting involved with anyone, hiding behind my political work—somehow I was showing him how wrong he was about me. But I was still letting him make my choices for me. I never wanted to be alone. I just didn't want to marry the person he said I had to and I didn't want to marry someone who saw me as a family name first and my wealth second. I didn't want to be used like he wanted to use me."

At that moment, Marie bumped into his leg, a book in her hand. He leaned down and picked her up, but his gaze never left Christine.

"That's all I wanted, too," she told him. "I didn't want to be a cog in my father's political machine and I didn't want Marie to be one, either. I just wanted to be accepted as I am. I just wanted to be good enough. And then I wanted to be good enough for you." She hung her head. Even now—with him right here—she couldn't believe he thought she was on the same level as he was.

"But you are," he said. Then, turning his attention to Marie, he said, "I need to talk to Mommy. Can you sit on the couch and read quietly?"

And, miracle of miracles, Marie nodded. He sat her down and she curled up on the couch, intent on her story.

Daniel turned his attention back to her. "You changed me, Christine. You're the one thing I never saw coming. I couldn't plan for you and the thought of not having a plan scares me—but not as much as the thought of not having you in my life. I always believed that I didn't fit anywhere but when I'm with you, I feel like I belong. I want to belong to you, Christine. Not to my grandfather and not to someone like Brian White. I don't want to live my life on the fringe of humanity anymore. I want to play with Marie in the park and have breakfast with you in the morning and I want to know that, at the end of the day—no matter what state or country I'm in—that I'm coming home to you."

One thing was clear. Daniel Lee had ruined her for anyone else. Even now—he was saying all the things she needed to hear. But there was one thing that still worried her. "I don't want this to be all because of some misguided notion that you're protecting me or that you owe it to me. And I don't want you to think that I only care for you because you're this elusive billionaire."

His eyes got wide. "Do you? Care for me, that is?"

"Oh, Daniel," she whispered, stretching up on her tiptoes and brushing her lips over his. "You ruined me for any other man. You stood by me when I needed you and you make things better. You're kind to my daughter and you make me feel like the woman I was always meant to be. How could I *not* love you?"

His arms went around her waist, holding her tight. "Do you really love me? Because I love you, too. I know it's quick, but I kept waiting for things to go back to normal again after you left and they didn't."

"Me, too," she said, her eyes stinging. "And they didn't."

"We can't go back," he said with a grin that got more confident by the second. "You changed me, Christine—for the better. You forgave me and I...this sounds crazy, but I think I've forgiven myself. This isn't about rescuing you. This is about having you by my side because I can't stand back and watch you walk away."

Her heart was pounding. Was this really happening? "So what are you saying? Do you want to try dating? Or..."

"I want more than that. I don't want you one night a week or lunch every other Thursday. I want you all the time. I want you *always*. Would you marry me, Christine?" From behind them, Marie trilled. Daniel smiled and, turning to the little girl, said, "Would you be my family, too, Marie?"

Christine gaped at him. *"What?"*

His grin sharpened and there it was, that intense feeling of being in Daniel Lee's sights. "Marry me, Christine. You're the strongest woman I know, but let me be the soft place you can land. Let me show you every day that you're the only woman for me. I want to adopt Marie. I want to be the man I think I was always meant to be. That's who I am when I'm with you."

Christine didn't even bother to blink back the tears. As far as proposals went, it was perfect—just like Daniel. Oh, she was under no illusions that he *was* perfect. But he was perfect for her and that was the most important thing of all. "Yes," she said, laughing and crying at the same time. "But promise me that you won't listen to *his* voice inside your head more."

With a huge grin on his face, he picked her up and spun her in a small circle. "The only voice I want inside my head is yours," he told her, lowering her back down to the ground and touching his forehead to hers. "Your voice is the only one that matters to me."

And then he kissed her and no one said anything at all for quite some time.

* * * * *

If you liked this story of a billionaire tamed by the love of the right woman—and her baby— pick up these other novels from Sarah M. Anderson.

*A MAN OF DISTINCTION
EXPECTING A BOLTON BABY
THE NANNY PLAN
HIS SON, HER SECRET
HIS FOREVER FAMILY*

Available now from Harlequin Desire!

***

And don't miss the next
BILLIONAIRES AND BABIES *story,*

*TEN-DAY BABY TAKEOVER
by Karen Booth.*

Available April 2017!

***

If you're on Twitter, tell us what you think of Harlequin Desire! #harlequindesire

MILLS & BOON®
Hardback – March 2017

ROMANCE

Secrets of a Billionaire's Mistress	Sharon Kendrick
Claimed for the De Carrillo Twins	Abby Green
The Innocent's Secret Baby	Carol Marinelli
The Temporary Mrs Marchetti	Melanie Milburne
A Debt Paid in the Marriage Bed	Jennifer Hayward
The Sicilian's Defiant Virgin	Susan Stephens
Pursued by the Desert Prince	Dani Collins
The Forgotten Gallo Bride	Natalie Anderson
Return of Her Italian Duke	Rebecca Winters
The Millionaire's Royal Rescue	Jennifer Faye
Proposal for the Wedding Planner	Sophie Pembroke
A Bride for the Brooding Boss	Bella Bucannon
Their Secret Royal Baby	Carol Marinelli
Her Hot Highland Doc	Annie O'Neil
His Pregnant Royal Bride	Amy Ruttan
Baby Surprise for the Doctor Prince	Robin Gianna
Resisting Her Army Doc Rival	Susan MacKay
A Month to Marry the Midwife	Fiona McArthur
Billionaire's Baby Promise	Sarah M. Anderson
Seduce Me, Cowboy	Maisey Yates

MILLS & BOON
Large Print – March 2017

ROMANCE

Di Sione's Virgin Mistress	Sharon Kendrick
Snowbound with His Innocent Temptation	Cathy Williams
The Italian's Christmas Child	Lynne Graham
A Diamond for Del Rio's Housekeeper	Susan Stephens
Claiming His Christmas Consequence	Michelle Smart
One Night with Gael	Maya Blake
Married for the Italian's Heir	Rachael Thomas
Christmas Baby for the Princess	Barbara Wallace
Greek Tycoon's Mistletoe Proposal	Kandy Shepherd
The Billionaire's Prize	Rebecca Winters
The Earl's Snow-Kissed Proposal	Nina Milne

HISTORICAL

The Runaway Governess	Liz Tyner
The Winterley Scandal	Elizabeth Beacon
The Queen's Christmas Summons	Amanda McCabe
The Discerning Gentleman's Guide	Virginia Heath

MEDICAL

A Daddy for Her Daughter	Tina Beckett
Reunited with His Runaway Bride	Robin Gianna
Rescued by Dr Rafe	Annie Claydon
Saved by the Single Dad	Annie Claydon
Sizzling Nights with Dr Off-Limits	Janice Lynn
Seven Nights with Her Ex	Louisa Heaton

MILLS & BOON®
Hardback – April 2017

ROMANCE

MILLS & BOON®
Large Print – April 2017

ROMANCE

A Di Sione for the Greek's Pleasure	Kate Hewitt
The Prince's Pregnant Mistress	Maisey Yates
The Greek's Christmas Bride	Lynne Graham
The Guardian's Virgin Ward	Caitlin Crews
A Royal Vow of Convenience	Sharon Kendrick
The Desert King's Secret Heir	Annie West
Married for the Sheikh's Duty	Tara Pammi
Winter Wedding for the Prince	Barbara Wallace
Christmas in the Boss's Castle	Scarlet Wilson
Her Festive Doorstep Baby	Kate Hardy
Holiday with the Mystery Italian	Ellie Darkins

HISTORICAL

Bound by a Scandalous Secret	Diane Gaston
The Governess's Secret Baby	Janice Preston
Married for His Convenience	Eleanor Webster
The Saxon Outlaw's Revenge	Elisabeth Hobbes
In Debt to the Enemy Lord	Nicole Locke

MEDICAL

Waking Up to Dr Gorgeous	Emily Forbes
Swept Away by the Seductive Stranger	Amy Andrews
One Kiss in Tokyo...	Scarlet Wilson
The Courage to Love Her Army Doc	Karin Baine
Reawakened by the Surgeon's Touch	Jennifer Taylor
Second Chance with Lord Branscombe	Joanna Neil